DAVID WEAVER PRESENTS

# CAPONE & CAPRI

## A BAD BOY ROMANCE

# JESSICA N. WATKINS

## DEDICATION:

This book is dedicated to each and every one of you that supported the Secrets of a Side Bitch series. I hope you enjoy!

**PLEASE READ:**

Secrets of a Side Bitch 4 ended with Jasmine and Omari's engagement in August of 2015. The epilogue fast-forwarded to their wedding in December 2016. Capone & Capri begins between those events, in January of 2016.

# CAPONE & CAPRI

## A BAD BOY ROMANCE

# PROLOGUE

## CAPRI

♫ *All my diamonds shine 'cause they really diamonds*
*Bad bitches in line, they be really tryin'*
*They ask me if I'm high*
*I say really really*
*Got money on my mind*
*I say really really* ♫

On New Year's Eve 2015, I found myself *finally* free. The new year looked so promising that I could literally feel my future success all over my skin as I held a shot glass tightly in the air. I smiled at my best friends and this guy, whom I'd just met, that was making my pussy leak with every wink that his sexy, dark, intimidating, and charming brown eyes sent my way.

"Okay! Are y'all ready?!"

Me and my best friend, Joi, smiled wide as we looked at Amiyah, our other best friend, who was waiting for us to respond.

Over the lyrics of Kevin Gates, I screamed, "Hell-motherfuckin'-yea!!"

Then me, Amiyah, and Joi, along with the guys, who had been buying our bottles all night, crashed our shot glasses together. They all screamed, "Congratulations, Capriiiiii!" as we took our fifteenth shot of tequila for the night.

Then me, Joi and Amiyah started to move our hips to the thunderous bass in the VIP section of Club Liv. We were drunk as fuck. In our heads, we looked like Black Chyna and Amber Rose twerking on some stage, but we actually looked like the mediocre hood versions of them as we rapped along with such dramatic gestures that you would have thought that *we* were all Kevin Gates himself.

♫ *Fresh with low mileage*
*I like 'em black*
*Pretty white teeth*
*Body unique*
*Booty on fleek*
*Jhene Aiko*
*Chewing her cheeks*
*Groceries please*
*You know that was for me*

*All my diamonds shine 'cause they really diamonds*
*Bad bitches in line, they be really tryin'*
*They ask me if I'm high*
*I say really really ♫*

The guys soon made their way behind us. Their hands nestled on our waists and their pelvises ground rhythmically against our asses to *Really Really.*

Me, Joi, and Amiyah didn't even know these guys. We met them while standing in line at Club Liv a few hours ago, excited about finally being able to step into the infamous Club Liv, which we'd heard mentioned by various rap artists in our favorite songs.

None of us had been to Miami before, and my recent completion of my x-ray tech program at Malcolm X College was a reason to finally come to South Beach, especially with it happening in conjunction with New Year's Eve. Even though my lame ass boyfriend, Maine, had been attempting to make my trip miserable since I got to Miami on Wednesday by constantly calling me, picking fights, and even going as far as claiming that the kids were sick, I had been having the time of my life! It was seventy-four degrees in comparison to the twenty-degree weather that I left back in Chicago. I had spent the last three days eating, drinking, and flirting without having to tend to my kids or Maine.

As we got in the line of Club Liv, I was feeling a joy that I hadn't felt in years. I had spent the last two years going to school full-time and taking care of two kids. Well, you can make that *three* kids since Maine had been acting like a big ass baby since I started school. It was like this nigga was intimidated by the fact that I was no longer going to be this unemployed chick that needed him to do everything for her. When I started school, I thought that he would be excited that I was finally doing something to better myself. And he acted like he was until I started proving that I was actually serious about something in my life for once. I didn't quit, as I had done hair school right after high school. I knew that since I had the kids, and Maine was so irresponsible and refused to grow up, I had to do something for myself. So I studied my ass off for two years while taking care of those kids, and I had finally graduated!

I was standing in line with my best friends, super geeked. We were dressed to impress and to bring the club down. Our faces were beat to death. Our virgin hair was curled flawlessly. And we were ready to party, but the line was long as fuck.

After thirty minutes of standing in line, a group of guys walked past us, looking and smelling like money. They skipped the entire line and went straight to the bouncer. They obviously had VIP. The bouncer told them that they could pick any woman in line to go in with them because of how many tables in VIP they had reserved. I thought it was hilarious how a lot of the chicks in line actually started begging and making sexual advances just to get in the club with them. To my surprise, the chocolate guy with the dreads pointed at the three of us and told us to come with them. Of course, we were game! Nobody wanted to stand in that long ass line, and every single one of these guys were fine as hell. Even though I was in a relationship, and so was Amiyah, we were about to have the time of our lives.

And that's what we had been doing for the last three hours.

Once we were inside of the club, we thought that the guys were going to ditch us, but they really did invite us to join them in their VIP section. We introduced ourselves to one another, but their names escaped me after the first three drinks. Each one of them immediately picked which one of us they wanted to claim for the night and started to cater to our needs. They got us our own bottles of Ciroc because they were drinking 1738.

Me and the girls felt like we were in a hood dream. We had spent this trip trying to find some guys to act up with, and I'll be damned, on our last night, we had lucked up. There had been many nice looking men on South Beach, but none of them were the hood niggas that we were used to back at home in Chicago. But these gangstas right here fit the bill to a T. So we allowed them to grab our waists, smile in our faces, and rub on our asses as we danced and drank their liquor.

It was the start of a perfect night... or so we all thought.

Now, three hours later, to say that I was drunk would be an understatement. I was so drunk that I had been letting the guy with the dreads rub his hard dick against my ass as we danced. I let him kiss my neck as he talked all type of shit in my ear. For some reason, I was so turned on by him. I had been faithful to Maine for the last three years, but I honestly could not wait for the moment that I got away from his negative, trying-to-bring-a-bitch-down face ass and got me some new dick. Sex with Maine had gotten so routine, and I longed for the day that me and him were no longer together, and I got me a new boo. I wasn't looking for another relationship, especially after being in one for three long, exhausting, irritating years. I was trying to get a team of niggas together to entertain me while I started my new career and took care of my kids.

"You know what to do with that, ma?" I heard him say into my ear.

I giggled but continued to grind my ass against him. I could feel his long, hard, thick steel on the other side of his Balmain jeans.

I smiled, trying to ignore the fact that my pussy was actually getting wet. The feeling of his lips against my neck as he talked shit to me turned me the fuck on. I knew I was so turned on so easily because I was drunk. But I still enjoyed the feeling of the deep bass in his voice rumbling against the sensitive part of my neck as he held my waist and ground, what felt like, eight inches against the back side of my mesh jumpsuit. I didn't need to know that he had a big dick; he was too much to take in already. On top of the fact that he was chocolate, fine, had bad boy written all over him, and had an absurd amount of tattoos, he had the nerve to have money and a big dick! *Lordt!*

To fuck with him further, I continued to roll my ass slowly and seductively against his pelvis. I felt his dick getting harder and harder. I knew I was asking for trouble. I didn't even know this dude, but that was exactly the situation that my drunk ass wanted. I was just looking to have a little fun in Miami and go back home to my regular, boring relationship until I had saved enough money from my new job to get my own place.

What happened in Miami was going to stay in Miami.

I heard his chuckle, which felt like a bottomless roar against my skin, as he threatened, "Man, shorty, you gotta stop throwing that thing back on me like that."

I looked back at him and smiled. "And if I don't?"

He simply chuckled again and replied, "Yea. A'ight."

Something about the way he threatened me turned me on even more. I had spent the last two years with a dude who played the part of a monster in the streets but was a bitch ass nigga in the crib. The fact that Maine was trying to do everything to bring me down turned me off and made him look like a bitch in my eyes. I'd been longing to be with a man that had swag, confidence, and dominance, and this man behind me with these dreads and thick ass beard was definitely all of that wrapped in sexy ass brown skin.

So instead of taking his threats seriously, I continued to fuck with him. As we continued to dance and take shots, I got the courage to cheat on Maine, courage that I hadn't been able to muster up in years. I allowed him to rub his hands all over my curves, surprised that he was attracted to my voluptuous curves and midnight-colored skin. I pressed my 36DD breasts to his chest every chance I got. The sexual tension was so thick between us; that, mixed with the way we vibed so well made me feel like I was indeed in a hood fairytale. I felt like at any moment, the clock would strike twelve and my glass slipper would turn back into Retro Jordan's.

I teased the man so much that he eventually grabbed my face and started to kiss me. I should have been ashamed. I should have pushed him away because I didn't even know him. But my drunk mind wanted all of the sober truth that his dick was telling me it wanted to give me as I allowed my hand to rub over its imprint as he kissed me.

The rest of my girls were so drunk that they didn't even see us making out like teenagers on the couch in the VIP section.

"C'mon."

I looked at him oddly while feeling my pussy literally pulsating and dripping. "Where are we going?"

"Don't ask questions. Just bring your pretty ass on."

And just like that, I allowed him to take my hand, pull me to my feet, and lead me out of VIP.

Amiyah and Joi were too busy in his friends' faces to even notice that he was taking me away. I clung to his hand as he led me out of VIP and through the thick, most likely unlawful, crowd of Club Liv.

Club Liv was notorious for its Sunday night party. Everybody was there. I had spotted so many rappers, models, reality stars, and actresses. Even a few of the Miami Heat players had been in the VIP section next to us, but I was so drawn to this particular guy that I hadn't even paid the celebrities any attention.

When he led me past the dance floor and down a hallway, I began to get even more curious. He passed the bathrooms and took me further into a dark, deep corner of the hall near an exit. Curiosity piqued even further when he opened a door to what looked like a closet, pulled me inside of the darkness of the room and closed the door.

"Where are—"

His lips on top of mine stopped my question. His tongue crashed into my mouth, and he started to suck my lips. I melted into his arms, not believing that this was how my trip was going to end.

It was the perfect fucking ending!

I allowed him to run his strong, big hands over my titties and shoulders until he was pulling down the straps of my jumpsuit. Seconds later, my jumpsuit was around my ankles, and I was standing completely naked in the darkness. However, I appreciated the darkness because my flaws were hidden.

If I had been sober, I would have stopped him. But none of the vodka that I had drunk that evening wanted him to. So

I allowed him to force me against a wall, then hoist me up and force my legs around his waist.

*Damn, this nigga can pick a big bitch up?* I thought with a smile on my face. I was five-foot-four and one-hundred and ninety pounds. Thick wasn't the word for me. I was more like a BBW that worked out here and there to keep my stomach from poking out more than my booty do.

He was so strong that my pussy leaked at his ability to hold me up with one arm as he unbuckled his belt and snatched down his jeans with the other.

He kissed me roughly just as I felt his hardness against my pussy, and I gasped as his thick length forced past my tightness.

"Gawd damn," he literally growled in response to the way I wrapped around his dick.

"Oh my God," was all that I could manage to moan.

I was so overwhelmed. Each stroke saw perfection. I wanted to call out his name, but my drunk ass had forgotten what it was.

The dick that he was giving me was award-winning. If I could have stayed in Miami a few more days just to get more of it, I would have. In addition, I couldn't believe that I was actually doing this shit. I couldn't believe that I was so fucking drunk and being a complete whore... but I loved it! I held onto him tightly, wrapped my arms around his neck and dug my nails into his sweaty skin as he penetrated me perfectly.

"Where the fuck is Capri?"

I jumped out of my skin when I heard Joi's voice. Her drunk ass was so loud that I recognized it above the music and the voices outside of the door that were standing in line outside of the bathroom.

He felt me getting nervous, felt me tense, so he held onto me tighter, grabbing my ass cheeks so tight that I felt his nails digging into my skin. He drove his dick so deep into me that I was scared that Maine would know that somebody had been tampering with his pussy.

*Pop! Pop! Pop!*

Suddenly, popping sounds could be heard faintly amongst the beats and lyrics of Young Gotti. At first, I ignored the faint noises, thinking nothing of it and focusing on the damn near blessed dick that this nigga was giving me. I bit my lip and rested my head back against the wall with my eyes closed tightly into slits, trying to take all of his length and width like a big girl as I felt the most orgasmic feeling that I'd had in years coming down.

But right after I heard the popping sounds, amongst our sexual moans and growls, screams could be heard outside the door. The music stopped as he and I jumped in fear. I began to shake uncontrollably, realizing that somebody was shooting in the club. Then I remembered that I had heard my girls nearby, but no longer could hear their voices.

I frantically pulled up my jumpsuit, and he quickly pulled up his jeans and snatched the door open. We both ran out. I was on his heels. I knew that he was looking for his friends, and I was looking for mine. But the frenzy of people running in all directions in fear made it hard for me to keep up with him. I had barely made it beyond the bathrooms when I heard a familiar voice call my name, "Capri!"

I frantically turned my head and was relieved when I saw Amiyah and Joi fighting their way through the hysterical crowd swarming me. As soon as we were within arm's reach, they grabbed me and pulled me towards the nearest exit, the one right next to the room that he and I had just left out of. Even in the frenzy, I thought of him as we neared the exit. I even turned back, but found nothing except people running, jumping, fighting, throwing glasses... and then there were more gunshots.

*Pow! Pow! Pow!*

We began to scream as our feet moved faster. I wasn't sure what would hurt us first; flying bullets or the stampede of people more concerned about saving their own lives than knocking somebody down and stepping on them. Fear replaced the sexual desires that I had just had moments ago. All I could think about was getting back to Chicago to my kids and, hell, even to Maine, if that meant that I had my life!

And just like that... my vacation was over.

# CHAPTER 1

## CAPRI

A month after leaving Miami, I found myself working at the University of Chicago Hospital as an x-ray tech in the emergency room department. I took x-rays of people with broken bones and fractured skulls after minor and major accidents. I loved my job for many reasons. For the first time in my life, I was making a decent amount of money. To be twenty-one years old, I was making twenty-seven dollars an hour. If I decided to go back to school to be certified as an ultrasound or MRI technician, I could possibly make fifty-to-sixty dollars an hour. That sounded like good money to take care of me and my kids, so that was the plan once I was able to get a reliable sitter.

I also liked my job because working twelve-hour shifts gave me the distance from Maine that I needed. Now that I was bringing in good money, he was *really* insecure about our relationship. Maine had spent the first three years of our relationship taking care of me and the kids. He literally bought everything that I needed, down to tissue and tampons. In exchange, I was very submissive to his needs. It was a good relationship until I started to grow up while his mentality stayed at the same immature level that thought a twenty-three-year-old man should still be selling nickel bags of weed on the corner and robbing people for a few hundred dollars. I was from the hood. I loved me a street nigga. Yet, I loved an intelligent, mature thug that was in the streets but knew how to establish something stable for his family's future so that he could eventually leave the streets. That was *not* Maine.

He thought he was *that nigga*. Maine felt like he ran shit when he ran nothing but that sorry, lame ass crew of dummies that followed him around. He was comfortable taking care of our household with nickel bag and robbery money, until I decided to be a better person. You would think that a man would like that his woman no longer wanted him to take care of everything and wanted to do something for herself, but that was not the case with Maine. He felt more secure when I was at home waiting for him to give me a few dollars so I could get a kitchen-weave. But I did not want to be that person anymore—for myself and for my kids. I had been saving as much as I could so that I could finally move out on my own and leave Maine to his low-budget hustling.

When I heard someone enter the break room, I tore my eyes away from my Facebook timeline on my mobile app. "Hey, Eboni!"

She shook her head and smiled as we met in the middle of the room and hugged. "I been lookin' for you since I clocked in, and yo' ass in here on that damn Facebook."

I giggled as I let her go. "I gotta know the T, girl."

She rolled her eyes. "Drama. That's exactly why I'm not on social media."

"Whatever, girl. I'm happy we're finally on the same shift!"

"I know right? How was your trip to Miami?"

I had met Eboni during clinicals here at the University of Chicago. Once we were done with clinicals and graduated, we were both able to get jobs in the emergency room, but hadn't worked the same shift since we started a month ago.

"The trip was fun." I kept it at that and smiled, but there was a nervousness running through my body as I thought about the trip; the nerves more so stemming from the thoughts of the guy that I had stupidly fucked and about how now my period hadn't come on since.

"It was just fun?" Eboni looked at me strangely as I sat there fidgeting nervously.

I forced myself to give her the watered down version of the trip. "We had a good time. It was nice to be on the beach. The strip is really fun, lots of people drinking and lots of men. We were so damn drunk the whole time, but it was great. You should go one day."

I really wanted to tell Eboni about the guy that I'd fucked at Club Liv. Not like I hadn't fantasized about him enough with Amiyah and Joi, but that dick and the scenario itself was so unbelievable that I wanted to share it with her. But though me and Eboni liked working together during clinicals, we weren't cool enough for her to know my dirt.

"Yea, some of my friends went there for New Year's Eve too, but it was me and Geno's first New Year's Eve together, so I wanted to do something a little more intimate. We are supposed to take a trip soon, though. Maybe I'll tell him that I want to go to South Beach," she said with the same smile that she always had on her face when she talked about her man, Geno.

"You're coming to my birthday party next month, right?"

"Hell yeah, I'll be there," I told her. "I wouldn't miss it for the world."

Eboni always went on and on about her family and crew. I felt like I knew all of them already, like they were my own friends and family, considering how much she talked about them, so I couldn't wait to meet them at her birthday party in a couple of weeks.

As my phone rang, Eboni excused herself, saying that she needed to start her shift.

"I'm right behind you as soon as I take this call."

It was Aunt Dawn calling. She had basically raised me, so was like a mother to me. Therefore, I answered quickly, "Hello?"

When I heard Auntie Dawn sigh before saying, "Hey," dread filled me as I sat at the breakroom table and braced myself.

"What's up, Auntie?"

She blew her breath sharply and spilled it, "I haven't been able to find your mother in a week. I need you to go to the area where she usually gets her drugs from and see if you see her."

I groaned, but before I could say anything, my aunt added, "I know, baby. I know you're tired of doing this. But I can't take my old ass over there fighting with her."

"She isn't answering the phone you got her?"

"No." She must have felt my reluctance, because she started to beg, "Please, Capri? You gotta go. We can't have her out there like that. If she's been gone for a week, she's probably out there real bad. And she ain't got no money, so there's no telling what she's doing to get some drugs."

She couldn't have been doing much. Back in the day, she used to sell pussy to get the money to support her habit. Now, that pussy was so dirty and cracked out that nobody would pay for it.

"Okay, Auntie. I'll go right after my shift is over."

"Okay, baby. Thanks."

I ended the call, mumbling to myself, "Yea whatever."

**\*\*\*\***

At the end of my shift, I hurried through the parking lot towards my Honda Civic. I swung the driver's door open and rushed inside, cursing my mother along the way. After twelve long hours in the ER, handling gunshot victims and sick and hurt kids, I did not feel like going to the hood looking for my dope fiend ass mama.

My mother had been giving me grief since the day she pushed me out of her walls. At that moment, she gave me to Auntie Dawn, who raised me. I wasn't born with any drugs in my system because my Auntie Dawn made my mother go to rehab the moment they found out she was pregnant with me. But when she gave birth to me, my mother started a downward spiral that she never recovered from. Even though she lived with my auntie, she often went missing for days and even weeks at a time. I never worried about her because I was tired of worrying about her at this point. I had done that enough when I was younger, to the point where she'd ruined my childhood. If my mother wanted to kill herself in the streets for some dumb shit like crack and heroin, then that was her business. I had kids to look after, and if I could be twenty-one and think of my kids, then at forty, my mother should have been able to as well.

But I loved my Auntie Dawn for stepping up to the plate, so whenever she said go, I went. Therefore, I reluctantly started the engine of my car and made my way to the southeast side. There was a gas station over there where my mother panhandled when she needed money for drugs, so I knew where to find her.

About fifteen minutes later, I was turning into the gas station on Commercial Avenue. Lo and behold, there she was, dressed in dirty jeans, a flimsy hoodie, despite the thirty-degree weather, and gym shoes that had holes in them and were obviously too big for her feet. I knew the shoes weren't hers. My auntie kept my mother in decent clothes. My mother had most likely sold her own shoes and found these somewhere in a dumpster.

I hopped out of the car, slamming the door. She was so fucking wasted that she hurried towards me asking, "Spare any change when you come out, lil' mama?"

My face contorted into irritation and disgust. My mother's face looked like struggle and defeat. This lady needed a fucking bath and a toothbrush.

"It's me, mama. Come get in the damn car," I spat with so much attitude. "Auntie Dawn been lookin' for you. Why haven't you been answering the phone?"

My mother sucked her teeth with disappointment, realizing who I was. "You got a couple dollars for me?"

"Yea, mama, whatever. As long as you get in the car."

Even though she went towards my car, I knew she was full of it. I would get her home, give her the dollars that I promised, and she would be gone again as soon as my aunt fell asleep.

As I followed her to the car, my nose turned up with disgust. I really didn't want her getting in my car, making it smell like garbage truck juice and any other funky ass shit she'd been sitting in for a fucking week.

As we climbed into the car, I screamed, "Roll the window down, damn!"

Just then, the sound of bass caught my attention because it was so loud. I turned to my left, and there was a blacked out Range Rover pulling into the gas station. My attention was then quickly grabbed by my mother, who was going through the change in my cup holder.

"Would you stop? Damn! I told you I'll give you some fuckin' money! *Do not* touch this change. I'm *not* playin' with you. This change is for the kids. They like to use it for the candy store after school."

"I need it for the candy store too," she snickered.

I sucked my teeth and started the engine, shaking my head with disgust.

Suddenly, I felt a familiar presence and my eyes fell out of the window onto a guy walking into the convenience store that was connected to the gas station. His back was turned as he walked into the store with a hood over his head, but the swag he owned felt as though it should have been familiar to me.

He reminded me of the guy that I'd met at Club Liv, who was a foggy memory to me. I couldn't remember his name or even what city he'd said he lived in. I had been so drunk that night that when I woke up the next morning, all I remembered was the incredible dick that he gave me in that dark closet... and the gunshots. I also remembered how good of a time we had. Our conversation was easy. He was funny as hell. I had been so comfortable around him that I would have liked to get to know him better outside of the liquor and the drunk sex. Unfortunately, when the mayhem in the club started, me, Amiyah and Joi ran to our rental car, jumped in and kept going. There'd been too much chaos in the parking lot for me to even stop to try to find him. Getting some guy's number was way less important than getting the fuck out of the way as the shooting flowed out of the club and into the parking lot. Fights started to break out as well, making it almost impossible to get out of the parking lot, but we managed. I woke up the next morning packing quickly and ready to get the fuck out of Miami, but in the back of my head, I was heartbroken that I didn't even have a chance to get his number.

I shook my head and tore my eyes away from the store. I then pulled off, thinking, *Damn shame. That was some good dick.*

Suddenly, a sickening smell swam into my mouth, forcing me to swallow it, and I damn near threw up. My neck snapped to the right, and I noticed my mother just sitting there as if she didn't smell like despair and death. "Didn't I tell you to roll the fuckin' window down?!"

# CAPONE

*Nah, that can't be shorty*, I thought to myself as I stood in the doorway of the store watching the Honda Civic speed away.

I shook my head as I paid for my gas and left out of the store, laughing at myself. *I need to get it together.*

It was crazy how that night with her in Miami had been on my brain ever since. Shorty was beautiful, and fucking that pussy had been *great*. But the couple of hours we had spent laughing and talking had stayed on my mind more than the pussy and her looks, surprisingly. That night, she was just supposed to be a jump off. I didn't even know where I was taking her when I led her out of VIP. I would have fucked her in a dark corner if I could; I was that drunk. Luckily for me, when I turned the knob to that door, it ended up opening up to the perfect secret spot that I needed to stash her away and get that pussy.

Even while I was fucking her, I didn't care that I couldn't remember her name. But the next morning, I woke up hating that I didn't get her number. All I could remember was the great time that we had. We kicked it like a motherfucker. Most women were all about my money. Even if they didn't know me personally, I think I smelled like dough because it was obvious that all of the bitches in Miami were on me for monetary value only. But this thick, phat booty goddess with skin the color of coal seemed like she saw me, not my money. I liked that shit. I would have at least liked to have her number so that we could get together in whatever city she lived in. A nigga like me traveled a lot now that I was getting money in ways that I had never dreamed of.

"What's wrong with you, homie?" Omari asked me as I climbed into my Range Rover and pulled off.

"That girl in that Honda looked like shorty from Miami." I was so stuck on the memory of her that I stared at the back of the Honda as it drove through a red light and out of my sight. "I don't think she said she lived in Chicago. That was something I would have remembered."

"*Nigga*, you don't even remember her name so how would you remember where she said she was from?"

I looked over to my right as I drove down Seventy-Fifth Street. "If you had been there with me like you were supposed to, I wouldn't be going through this. You would have made sure that I got her info. You would have never let me slip like that."

Omari should have definitely been in the building during that epic ass trip to Miami for New Years, but he had already made some romantic, cake boy plans with Jasmine. Knowing how much he loved his girl, I knew I couldn't talk him out of canceling his plans with wifey to spend New Year's Eve with his boys. Plus, Jasmine would have never let that shit go down anyway.

I had gathered my closest homeboys from our organization, and we hit the streets of South Beach. Hood niggas like us had never been out of the city, so I treated all of my guys to the biggest suite at the most lavish, five-star hotel. Shit went down in a major way. The entire weekend was epic as fuck. We had so many women in and out of our suite that certain things happened that we could never even repeat or were too ashamed to. The only thing that stood out from that weekend was the moment I met that dark chocolate shorty. She was as black as Omari, but her skin was damn near glowing, like some African goddess that my history teachers used to try to make me study about in school.

Even though my eyes were back on the road, I could feel Omari's teasing grin as I heard him ask, "You really feeling shorty like that?"

I shot him a cynical sneer real quick and put my eyes back on the road as I turned onto Stony Island. "You know I'm feeling her like that. I've been talking about her since I got back from Miami."

"I mean, I knew you felt like you had a good time that night and you thought the pussy was so good, but the way you looking right now is like you in love or something."

I turned the corner of my upper lip up in disgust. "In love? Hell nah."

Omari knew better. Since the moment he met me three years ago, when I was seventeen going on eighteen, he knew the only thing he'd ever seen me falling in love with was the streets and this dope money. I rarely even fucked these thots more than a few months, maybe six, if the pussy was good. I was a young nigga with money... lots and lots of fucking money. Me and Omari's organization had quadrupled since the moment we started it. I had no time to focus on love; I was focused on this bread.

Plus, I knew nothing about love. I wasn't a man like Omari who had been in long-term relationships and knew what it felt like to have a woman's dedication and loyalty. I came from a mother who loved the shit out of me, and even a father who was in my life. But I had never met a woman who ever brought this feeling they called "love" out of me. No woman I had ever met in these streets exemplified anything worth what my parents taught me to bring home, so I never did.

Nevertheless, I had thought about that girl from Club Liv every fucking day since we had to run up out of that motherfucker after my crazy ass boy, Rico, started shooting at a nigga for knocking over his bottle of 1738. I still chuckled when I thought about running back into that club and seeing Fred's crazy ass standing in VIP with a gun in his hand, ready to have Rico's back with whatever. Then the guy that Rico had shot at had niggas with him that came back bussin'. Our gun play poured out into the damn parking lot. The shit was crazy. We got the fuck up outta there so fast, and I'd had to dip so serious, that I didn't even have the chance to go find shorty to get her information.

"You might not be in love, my nigga, but you definitely 'in like.'"

I shrugged my shoulders. "It don't matter either way. I'll never see her again."

# CHAPTER 2

## MAINE

"Bruh, I don't wanna do this."

*You gotta be fucking kidding me*, I thought as I asked Shug, "Are you serious?"

I didn't need this shit. I had to get to this money. There was no question about it. Capri was going to leave me at any moment. I knew she was. For years, I had held on to her only because I was her bread and butter. I didn't like the feeling that I only had her by the purse strings, but I knew what she was worth. She was a beautiful woman, and any nigga would love to take care of her, so having her by my side in any way was good enough for me. But now, even my money wasn't good enough. She wanted a stable man, a provider; not some nigga like me who *barely* survived by committing petty crimes. I had been too stubborn to ever admit that I would look at niggas in the hood that was on and envy how comfortable they were in foreign cars with women beside them dressed in labels that he had showered her with. I wanted that for me and Capri, but for so many years, my hustle had been petty, bringing in minimal cash that was only enough to barely pay our bills... until now.

"Yeah, I'm serious, man. These my people. I feel bogus as fuck for doing this to them."

I looked at Shug like he was crazy. "These your people? *I'm* your fuckin' people. You met this nigga in high school. Yea, y'all might have smoked weed together and kicked back a few times, but that was about it. Who been holding hold you down, hittin' licks with you, been in these streets with you? That was *me*, nigga. *I'm* your peoples. *I'm* your family. Fuck this nigga."

Shug shook his head with confusion in his eyes. He still wasn't too sure about this, but I didn't have time for a scary nigga thinking about motherfuckers who already had money,

I pushed the driver's door open and got out, knowing that Shug would follow me anyway. He always did what I told him to do. We had been in these streets trappin' for years together. He knew that no matter the risk, this was the move, and he needed to have my back.

As we walked up to the trap house that we were about to rob, I felt my adrenaline rushing with excitement. We were about to run up on niggas that Shug hung with on a regular basis, one being a homie from high school. That's how I knew how much work they had in inside; Shug would always come telling me about it. They sold a lot of dope out of here, so there was a lot of product and cash inside. I needed all of it to get on for my family's sake. I was ready to do what I had to to make sure that Capri knew that I was that nigga, no matter how much money she was making. Even if I had to take a nigga's work, money, or life, I was ready to do it.

As we crept slowly up the porch steps, I could see hundreds of thousands of dollars, considering the product we were about to take, in my future. So, I had no reason to be scared and all reasons to be fearless.

But even knowing that we were about to be thousands of dollars richer, Shug was literally sweating bullets. It was cold as fuck, damn near thirty degrees outside. Therefore, he had no reason to be sweating other than the fact that he was scared like a little ass kid. Admittedly, this was out of the norm for us. We usually stuck up regular people and small-time dealers, ran credit scams here and there, stole cars for cash, shit like that. But we had never hit a big lick like this; robbing the spot of the huge, well-known organization, DBD.

Still, I didn't feel that there was a single reason to be scared. I was counting the money in my head that I knew was about to be at my fingertips as we got to the front door of the crib.

I snatched my gun from my waist and shot the door open so fast that Shug didn't have time to react. I didn't even think; the first nigga I saw, who was jumping off of the couch as I charged into the crib, got two to the chest.

I watched his eyes bulge as he hit the floor, clutched his chest and began to bleed out. I recognized him by memory from all the things Shug had told me about him. It was his homie, Fred.

"Maine! What the fuck?!" Shug was freaking out behind me. I had just killed one of his boys but fuck that; I was getting to the money.

"Go grab the shit," I told Shug's whining ass.

I didn't have a chance to see if he was still behind me before a light-skinned motherfucka came charging out of the back room blazing! I was on point with the trigger and hit that nigga straight in the forehead. He went down before he could aim any of his bullets directly at me.

"Shug, we gotta get the fuck outta here! Hurry the fuck up!" My silencer on my gun had not attracted any attention at first, but this nigga dying on the floor had probably alerted the neighbors. Even though this was a high crime area, somebody was going to call the police soon. Though this was a trap house, Shug had told me how the niggas who ran this shit, Capone and Omari, were really good to the neighborhood. They looked out for the people on the block so that, in turn, they would look out for them. So, I knew that someone probably heard the gunshots and were calling the police right at that moment.

I charged through the house looking for Shug, who I found in the living room, desperately looking at his boy bleed out. Fred was unconscious, so he was for sure dead. Shug needed to care more about the dope that he had grabbed, which I knew was in the large black trash bag that he had in his left hand.

I snatched him by his arm and demanded, "Let's ride out."

I literally had to pull Shug towards the front door. His feet were like cement as he stared at death entering Fred's body.

As we ran out of the crib and towards the 2001 Yukon we'd stolen an hour ago in order to do this dirt in, I knew Shug felt some type of way about this shit. I also knew that I was going to have to deal with him before his conscience led him to deal with me.

## CAPONE

"Yeeeees, Capone. That's it, baby. Give me that dick."

*I wish this bitch would shut the fuck up*, I thought as I cringed with irritation and tried hard not to allow her high, squeaky voice to cause my dick to go down.

To shut her up, I lowered my body on top of hers and rested on my elbows. While continuing to give her this dick with long, deep, thick strokes, I used one hand to cover her mouth and the other to slightly choke her. Alicia liked that rough shit, so even though her moans were now muffled, she was giving me even more dramatics, and I could feel her pussy dripping all over the condom that was wrapped around my dick.

I closed my eyes tightly, trying to focus on anything that would make me bust faster so I could get the fuck out of this chick's crib. It wasn't that I wasn't into Alicia; I just wasn't *that* into her. We only fucked at times like this; one or two in the morning after I had been drinking and trapping all day and needed to bust a nut. I never even took her out, and only fucked her maybe once a month since meeting her three months ago.

As I swam in Alicia's pussy, my thoughts went to my black beauty that had been on my mind all day. It was crazy how I was so fascinated by her that I actually thought I had seen her at the gas station earlier that day.

As I thought of her, I felt my body starting to finally come close to an orgasm, so I continued to think about *her*. I couldn't remember her name, but I could remember her beautiful face, the way her natural, juicy curves felt in my hands, and the way my dick felt at home when I drunkenly slipped up in her.

As I continued to muffle Alicia's voice, I forced myself to remember how my black beauty's voice sounded in my ear as she moaned into it while I'd tried to give her the best drunk dick that I could. I imagined the shooting never happening, therefore being able to continue fucking the shit out of her and finishing her off the way that I wanted to, then ending it with a kiss and an exchange of information so that we could do that shit over and over again. It wasn't just the sex that I wanted to do again. I wanted to repeat the conversation, the laughs; all of the things that made me feel more comfortable with her than I had with any woman that I'd had in my short life. It was crazy that I wanted to be around her again just so that I could get that feeling back that her presence gave me. It was a feeling that I had never felt before, and I had been chasing it ever since.

I kept imagining her to the point that Alicia was screaming out in good agony and sweet torture as I plunged into her pussy fast, hard, and consistently...until I finally came, opened my eyes, realized that it was still just Alicia, and rolled over in disappointment.

*I'm trippin',* I thought. *Why am I thinking about shorty like this?*

I didn't get it. I didn't do shit like this. I didn't fixate on women and think about doing anything with them other than fucking them. It definitely didn't happen with women I didn't even know, women whose names I didn't know, whose number I couldn't even call. I was actually even considering going back to Miami, to Club Liv, and doing my own investigation just to find her. Me and Omari had enough connections that it could happen, and I was actually thinking about going that route until I heard my phone ringing and was forced to focus on bigger matters.

It was Omari calling me. So, even though I had just bust a nut, my mind was on other things, and it was two o'clock in the morning, I answered the phone anyway.

"What up, boss?"

Even though me and Omari were partners, I still called him boss. I was the one that taught him the street game, but because he was not raised in the streets, and was older and wiser than me, he had taught me more than he knew. Because of him, I was no longer some young kid selling heroine to crackheads out of some dirty ass trap house for a nigga who didn't give a fuck about putting me on. Now, I was my own man, pushing weight to the same niggas that wouldn't put me on. I owed that to Omari, so he would always get much respect from me.

"Yo', man... Um..."

The hesitation in his voice had me shook. Omari had been through a lot of shit since I met him. His girlfriend and daughter were killed by his side bitch. He had been through a lot of sadness, and luckily Jasmine brought a lot of happiness back into his life, along with his son, Jamari. I hadn't heard this type of sadness in his voice in a long time, so his hesitation had me shook as I sat straight up and asked him, "What happened?"

His continued hesitation scared the fuck out of me. I hopped out of bed so fast that Alicia looked at me with worry. I was throwing on my clothes as I shot continuous questions at Omari before he could get a word in.

"Is it Eboni? Is Jamari okay? Is Jasmine cool?"

Finally, Omari spoke up. "The spot over east got hit..." A deep, long sigh followed, as he then told me, "It's Fred and Rico..."

Now, I was running out of Alicia's house with no shirt on and my Balenciaga shoes untied. Alicia was calling after me, but I ignored her as I heard Omari say, "Fred made it through. He's in surgery, but... Rico's gone."

As I hopped in my Range Rover and slammed the door, I could see Alicia standing in the doorway of her house. Enraged, I punched the steering wheel, not believing that I was feeling yet another set of emotions that I had never felt in my life in such a short time. Even though I had lost many friends to the streets, and had even watched as Omari suffered the loss of his closest loved ones, it was never the same as going through it for yourself. This shit here hurt like a motherfucker. Fred was my homie. He had worked for me and Omari since we opened our first spot in the suburbs. I hurt for him too and prayed he pulled through, but I had grown up with Rico. Like Omari, me and Rico were like brothers. He was two years younger than me, but we'd lived next door to each other for most of our lives. And once he was a little older, I was putting him on, like Omari had put me on.

Omari continued to tell me the details of what happened as I sped through the streets of Chicago towards the hospital Fred had been rushed to. Omari said that their bodies had been found by a neighbor who saw two dudes run out of the crib, jump into a Yukon and speed off. The neighbor knew us and what we did, so he made sure that the crib was clean before calling 9-1-1 and then calling Omari. Fred had gotten one of his baby mamas to rent the house out in her name, so she would have to answer any of the police's questions. Her loyalty wasn't in question. She would never snitch.

We didn't know how much them niggas had gotten away with because it was too soon to even go on the block. Homicide detectives would have it occupied for hours. But I didn't care how much they'd taken. I could only think of having to tell Rico's mother that he was gone and looking in her eyes—eyes which I knew would look towards me with guilt because I had put him in this situation. But she didn't have to put the guilt on me; I was already putting it on myself as I thought about living the rest of my life without my brother.

Whoever had done this was going to pay. Omari and I never had issues like this. The only nigga we had come against us was Ching, and he was now retired from the game and was somewhere in the suburbs living off of the money he had stashed away while dealing after beating his murder case. Since then, DBD, Death Before Dishonor, never had issues like this. We ran a smooth organization based on honor, respect, and loyalty. We ran a tight ship, and we didn't let new people in just so we wouldn't have issues like this. The whole hood took care of us because we took care of them. This had to be some goofy ass niggas trying to come up on some luck. But that luck was about to end because it was now war.

## CAPRI

"Please explain to me why you are calling me at seven o'clock in the morning."

I chuckled at Amiyah as I drove through a dark cloud of my fucked up reality towards my job.

I couldn't believe my fucking life.

"It's an emergency. I really need to talk to you. Is Shug around you?"

Amiyah sucked her teeth as she yawned. "Hell no. He's sleep on the couch."

I laughed. "You made him sleep on the couch? What he do this time?"

"Came in the house at six in the morning acting weird as hell and would not tell me where he had been. I just know he was fucking some bitch."

"He was with Maine at some point because Maine left around midnight to pick him up, but Maine came in about two this morning. I wish his ass would have stayed out until six, though, or hell, never came back."

That was real talk. Any time in the house without Maine was well spent. It was the only time that I could have peace in my own damn house. But that wouldn't last for much longer. By the time I got paid again, I would have enough to put a deposit and first month's rent down on a nice place for me and the kids. Then, I would be free of Maine and his immaturity.

"Well, Shug is getting his ass whooped as soon as he wakes up. I don't play that shit. He's supposed to beat the sun home, and he know that." Then she grunted. "I just *know* he was with some thot ass bitch. I hate that nigga."

She didn't hate him that much. Amiyah and Shug had been together as long as me and Maine had. Being best friends, Shug was always around while Maine was courting me. Since Amiyah and Joi were my best friends, they were always around as well, but Joi acted too bougie to give a street nigga like Shug some play. She never gave Shug's fine ass a second look, but Amiyah was on it. For years, Amiyah and Shug had the typical hood love affair— dramatics, drama and bitches—but to this day, she felt like that shit was the norm, so she steadily put up with it.

"But what's the T? Why you got me up so early in the morning?" Amiyah asked. "Spill it."

I groaned. I hated to even say it out loud. "I'm pregnant."

Amiyah gasped, and suddenly she didn't sound sleepy anymore. "Are you fucking serious? How you want to leave the nigga, but you over there getting knocked up by him?"

I reluctantly replied, "I... I don't know... if it's his baby."

"The fuck do you mean?!" Amiyah asked excitedly.

This was some real good, hot tea from me. I didn't cheat on Maine. Even though I had wanted to for years, I never did because me and Maine's issues weren't other women. I had never caught him up with a woman or anything, so I had respected him by doing the same. Our issues were more emotional and developmental: Maine was emotionally unstable and needed to develop into a grown ass man.

"When did you get you some, girl?" Amiyah asked.

"Club Liv," I reminded her.

"Oh shit! Are you fucking serious? You didn't use a rubber?"

I cringed, my stupidity becoming even more apparent as she scolded me. "I don't even remember. I was so drunk," I confessed.

"If you don't remember, it might not be his. It might be Maine's."

"But I can't take that chance! And I don't want no damn baby by Maine! I'm trying to leave this nigga, not make a family with him!"

"So get rid of it. Problem solved."

This was an easy fix to Amiyah but not me. She made it sound so simple, but it wasn't. I had longed for the chance to have another baby after the last opportunity was taken from me. Who the fuck was I to kill a child after begging God for another chance to have one?

"I know," I said reluctantly.

However, in some cases, termination was necessary. This was one of those cases for me. "But I have to do it fast. It's like Maine finds out everything about me. I can't sneak and do shit, and he knows my cycle. He'll notice if I don't come on my period on time."

"I got you. I'll make you an appointment while you're at work."

I sighed with disappointment. I didn't want to do this. My heart hurt as I pulled into a parking space near the hospital. "Thanks, friend."

I hung up with a sigh of relief. I hated to do this shit, but I really couldn't remember nothing about that night at Club Liv, except the fact that that man had been the best I'd ever had. I couldn't remember whether he protected himself or not, and I definitely didn't want a baby by a stranger or Maine, so I had to take care of my business.

# CHAPTER 3

## CAPRI

Amiyah had kept her promise. Three days later, I was walking out of the clinic with my best friends right by my side. I was the one that had just done the most ratchet thing I had ever done in my life. I had just gotten rid of a baby because I didn't know who the father was, the choices being between one man that couldn't get his shit together at the age of twenty-five, and another man that I couldn't even get in contact with because I didn't bother to get his name or phone number before or after I fucked him, on the first night that I met him. I had just done what I swore to God I would never do if he gave me one more chance of conceiving. I was the one that should have looked like shit, but Joi was the one with her mouth poked out.

"What's wrong with you?" I asked as we walked towards Joi's 2015 Lincoln Navigator.

At the age of twenty-one, Joi was a lot more successful than me and Amiyah. That was mainly because she had two parents who took very good care of her. We had all attended the same elementary school, but once her father became a lawyer, she moved out of the hood on the south side and into a big ass house in the suburbs. She went to a much better high school than me and Amiyah, and she was currently going to college. Her parents would have rather she had gone to some Ivy League school in New York or something, but Joi couldn't imagine our crew separating, especially after one of our members had just been taken away from us. So she begged her parents to allow her to stay and attend DePaul University on the north side of the city. Her parents made sure that she was well taken care of, as long as she got good grades in school. Her life was a complete contradiction to the one that Amiyah and I were living.

I had no idea why her lip would be poked out, but I should have known that it was for the usual reasons.

"Girl," she sighed as she turned her engine. "Reggie hasn't called me back. I've been calling him all morning."

This was a typical complaint from Joi. No matter how good of a life she had, according to her, her life was miserable because she could never find the right man. She thought herself too classy for a hood nigga, but she couldn't get a regular man to act right. Sometimes I felt like if she just let her guard down and stopped requiring a ring as soon as she gave a man some pussy, she wouldn't be pushing them away so fast.

Oftentimes, she talked shit about the type of men that me and Amiyah had, but ... *we had one.*

"Damn, give the man a chance. Maybe he's busy... Stalker," Amiyah teased.

I was in the backseat suffering from serious cramps and guilt that kept me from laughing like I wanted to.

"Fuck you, Amiyah."

"Hey, it's true. You steady callin' that man. You gon' push him away steady blowing his phone up."

"I'm fucking him. I should be able to blow his phone up."

"But you're not his girl."

"So? What's that mean?"

I just sat in the back seat shaking my head at how naive she was. No matter the college education her parents paid for, she was a dummy when it came to the streets. She didn't realize that even a man with a nine-to-five gave a woman a hard time. You can give a man some pussy all you want to, but it didn't mean he was going to wife you.

As I sat in the back seat listening to Joi's bullshit, I scrolled through text messages that I missed from Maine while under sedation.

**9:00am:** *What are you doin'? I been callin' you all mornin'.*
**9:12am***: You on some bullshit.*
**10:15am***: You been actin' so shady lately.*
**10:30am***: Fuck you then.*

I didn't need this on top of the fucked up feeling I already had about what I had just done. But this was typical, insecure, bullshit for Maine. Even though, yes, I was on bullshit, I had told his crazy ass that I was at work. There was no way that he could call to see if I was actually at work because it wasn't like I had a desk or something. He could only get in contact with me by my cell phone. Therefore, I was sure that he had no idea what I was doing. It was just his insecurities because he could see in my eyes that I was two steps from leaving him. I was one paycheck away from getting the hell away from his immature, halfway hustling ass. I knew that I was barely any better than Maine, considering the way that I had acted in Miami, but I had my reasons. I was tired of feeling suffocated for the last two years by a man that didn't want to grow along with me. I wanted more for me and my kids than living off of petty hustle money with no insurance, no benefits, and no college fund. I wanted more for them than what I had growing up. It was me and Maine's responsibility to give them that, but he wasn't mature enough to appreciate what I wanted for our family.

I could no longer blindly follow him into a life of petty crime that would only lead him to death or jail.

****

When I got home, I was able to quiet the kids in the living room with the most candy they'd ever seen at one time and Frozen. The kids were silent, but my biggest child was crying like a baby. Maine's text messages were now verbal and all in my face as I lay in bed waiting for my pain pills to kick in. I just wanted the pain in my stomach and heart to go away,

"You losing respect for me," Maine spat.

I frowned as I stared at the ceiling. "What are you talking about?"

"You won't even answer the phone when I call."

"I was *at work*."

"Yea right."

"Yea right?! What the fuck are you bitching about?"

"Bitching? See? That's what the fuck I'm sayin'! I'm a bitch now?"

He sounded like a bitch just asking that question, but I held in my giggle. "I didn't call you a bitch."

"You think because you make more money than me now that I'm a bitch ass nigga?"

"I didn't say that—"

"Because I'm 'bout to be on, believe that," he barked with his chest poked out. "A nigga 'bout to be poppin'. *Shiiid.* I done came up."

"Came up?" I taunted him. "That's what I'm talking about. I can't give my kids a life off of a fucking come up."

I could see him smiling arrogantly as he stared at himself in the mirror on our dresser. "I can with this one."

I was disgusted, staring up at the ceiling with my lip curled upward in anger.

It was a shame that Maine was the total opposite on the inside than what he appeared to be on the outside. Maine was a little over six feet tall, but his swag was that of a nigga over seven feet. Confidence oozed out of his brown skin and light brown eyes. He had grown out his fade into a curly, short length afro that was encased in a lining so crisp that it almost looked like it hurt. His beard game was on point; it was as luxurious and shiny as his hair, and he was growing it into a length long enough to play with. When I first met him, and he actually pursued me, I thought I was the luckiest bitch sitting at the bus stop. I had been happy to leave the bus stop and hop into his Impala. I thought that beyond his good looks, he was the bad boy that every good girl dreamed of. He was the exact man that my Aunt Dawn wouldn't want me to be with, so I was very turned on by him.

That only lasted as long as I was the young girl who needed him to eat, to breathe, to feed my kids. As soon as I wanted to better myself, his bad boy persona turned into a bitch.

There was no need for continuing to argue with Maine. He was stuck in the mind frame that I would never be able to change. I wasn't a hypocrite; I knew where I'd come from. That was why I'd accepted the things Maine had to do to get money all this time. But if Maine had at least been a big time hustler who was investing his money and flipping it into something that could legally take care of his kids for the long run, while being the responsible man that my children needed to have in their life to look up to, I would respect him and his hustle, and I would stay with him. But money can't teach a boy how to be a man. I knew that no matter this come up he was referring to, he was still going to be the same man that he was looking at in the mirror.

# CAPONE

"You want some water? Hell, a drink?"

I lay across Rachel's bed face down, unable to move, so I simply shook my heavy head slowly. That was the position I had been in for three days, ever since I learned that Rico had been killed. I was ready to wage war against anybody who had pulled the trigger and on anybody involved in the robbery. Even though Fred was still alive, he was barely clinging to life, unresponsive, and couldn't tell us anything. The only clue we had to who had done this was the neighbor that had found their bodies. He had caught a glimpse of the two dudes as they ran out of the house. We had done all we could to try to get him to recall if he knew or recognized them. Yet, all he knew was that he recognized one of them from hanging out at the house sometimes, but was not a part of our crew.

I wanted to come right out and tell Rachel, "Hell no." I wanted to spit at her, "How can I eat or drink knowing that my brother is about to be buried in four days? How can I get drunk when I'm already so fucking mad that I'm ready to kill anybody?" Me being drunk would only put everyone's lives in danger around me, including hers.

I didn't say any of that though because I had more respect than that for Rachel. She had been by my side since the moment she called me and heard the pain in my voice. She had rushed over to my condo and refused to leave, despite me angrily insisting that she did. She was there to make sure that I didn't hurt myself or anybody else because of the guilt and anger simmering and boiling over inside of me.

Rachel was a chick that I had been fucking off and on for about two months. To me, she was just a cool chick with some good pussy, but nothing more than that. She, on the other hand, probably thought that I was her boyfriend. Though we had never put a title on what we were, I knew that I was the only man that she was sleeping with. Since she was four years older than me, she thought she could persuade me into a relationship with sex and the fact that she had her own. But there was no persuading a nigga like me. I had never been in a committed relationship, and there wasn't shit she could do to make her the first woman to get me to settle down.

However, she had been at my place for three days trying to show me otherwise. Even in my anger and sadness, I was not convinced.

As I lay on the bed, oddly, I thought about my black beauty in Miami and wished that I could be in her arms instead of Rachel's, who clearly had a motive. It was crazy how, no matter how hard she tried, Rachel couldn't make me feel better. But there was something about being in my black beauty's arms in that smoky, loud club that had made me feel more calm and at peace than I had felt in my whole life. And I needed to feel that shit right at this very moment.

# CHAPTER 4
*-a month later -*

## CAPRI

"Are you sure you're going to make it to my party tonight?" Eboni asked me.

She watched me questionably as I sat at the table in the breakroom. I had a fucked up attitude. Over the last month, I had been able to bury the guilt of my abortion, ignore it and move on.

This current attitude was because of Maine. I had had it since Monday, when Maine went through my phone and found text messages from real estate agents sending me listings for available apartments in the city. He officially knew that I was leaving him and was sending me through hell. I had tried to convince him that I was just looking and wasn't sure that I was leaving, just for the sake of having peace in the house until I left. But he was not buying that. He spent his every waking moment trying to figure out what nigga I was leaving him for. He never once acknowledged that I had been drilling into his head for months that he was not the man that I needed in my life for me or my kids, and maybe *that* was the reason I would be leaving. He didn't hear any of that; he was too self-absorbed to even acknowledge his own flaws. Instead, he wanted to convince himself that it was because of another man.

I was close to leaving the house all together and staying with a family or friend. But my options were few. Most of my family lived in Wisconsin where my mother was born and raised. My Aunt Dawn moved to Chicago with her husband when he got a good paying job in the city years twenty-two years ago. My mother moved with her. I regret that she did, though. This city was what had gotten her high and never allowed her to come down. Aunt Dawn's husband passed away ten years ago, and there was more than enough room in her house for me and the kids, but I would be damned if I stayed in the same house as my thieving, trifling ass mother. She would not hesitate to sell anything that was not bolted down to the floor for drugs. I had worked too hard saving my money just for her to steal it and get high with it.

Amiyah's house was just as much of a war zone as mine was. Ever since that day that Shug came home acting funny, he had not changed at all. He was still being uptight, and Amiyah felt like he was hiding something from her. She was sure that he was cheating and was obsessed with finding out with who.

Joi had been standoffish, but I was sure that it was because she was up under one of those dudes that she was trying to force to marry her.

"Girl, I'll be fine," I told Eboni. "You've been talking about that party for weeks now. I'm not going to let Maine make me miss that party."

"Okay, girl. Is he coming with you?"

I frowned in disgust. "Hell no."

Eboni smiled. "Good because there will definitely be some eye candy with money in the building. A few of Geno's friends will be there, and Omari and Capone are coming with their crew."

"Your baby's daddy is coming to a party where your boyfriend will be at?"

Even though she had told me over and over again that her baby's daddy and boyfriend were so cool, I thought it was weird that they actually hung out together.

"Yeah, Omari and his fiancé, Jasmine are coming. We're one big happy family," she said with a smile that I envied because I knew that it was the product of having a good man.

Eboni often went on and on about Geno and how he was so loving in a man's man kinda way. He had come into her life and took over in a way that every woman longed for.

I envied that shit so much that I wanted to smack her happy ass and high-five her at the same time.

I shook my head saying, "You guys are so fucking weird...but I love it."

She smiled even brighter as she headed for the break room door. "I love it too, girl. See you later...and dress cute! Show that ass off! It's gon' be some money in the building!"

# CAPONE

"Are you sure you should be going to this party tonight?" Jasmine asked me.

She was looking at me with fear in her pretty eyes as I stood pacing the kitchen in Omari's house.

My sadness about seeing my boy, Rico, being lowered into the ground had now turned into anger because Fred had woken up. Though he was groggy and in and out, he had said one name: Shug. Memories of the night were foggy to Fred, but he remembered that, though Shug was not the shooter, he was definitely one of two dudes that had robbed us that night. Fred didn't recognize Shug's accomplice, however.

I didn't know Shug personally, but I had heard some of the guys mention him being at the trap house in random conversation. Rico had definitely mentioned Shug to me a few times because he was one of Rico's close friends from school. I couldn't believe this motherfucker had broken every street code by doing some shit like this. I was going to find that snake if it was the last thing that I did and torch the fuck out of him before I killed him.

"Capone, my nigga, you know I feel you on this," I could hear Omari saying behind me as he stood in the doorway of the kitchen. "I got your back in whatever you wanna do. But tonight is also a celebration. Fred is going to make it, and that's a reason to go party. You know that's what he would want. Rico too. They would be right next to us popping bottles if they could."

My nigga was right. If Rico and Fred were able to, they would be at Eboni's party turning the fuck up. We had all become so close because Omari forced that shit down our throats. Family and loyalty were important to him because he was making up for the disloyalty to his family that he felt had caused their murders. He made sure that the crew and our significant others spent holidays and many weekends together. We were all like blood, even though there was no relation between us. Even Eboni's boyfriend, Geno, was becoming an intricate part of our circle, and he was now a faithful buyer of our product as well.

Fred and Rico would not have missed this party, so I couldn't miss it... for them.

Even though I agreed mentally, I was too much of an asshole to show any emotion but hate, so I spat, "Whatever," and headed out of the side door which lead to the garage, knowing that Jasmine and Omari were following me.

I was only wearing a hoodie and jeans, a huge downgrade from the high end, expensive labels that I would usually be wearing to an event like this, but my jewelry game stayed on point. I never took my diamonds off of my wrists, out of my ears, or from around my neck. Yet, my gear was in no comparison to how Jasmine and Omari were stepping out tonight. As I climbed into the back of Omari's ride, I would have commended Jasmine on how nice she looked in that bandage dress. Then I would have kept the fact that her curves were poppin' to myself because I knew Omari would have flipped, with his overprotective ass.

Even my nigga Omari was stuntin' in Balmain and Gucci from head to toe, and his locs had me sick with envy because his had grown damn near to his waist, when mine were only a couple of inches past my shoulder.

All of our homies and family were going to be at the Promontory in Hyde Park. Geno had rented out the whole spot for Eboni's birthday. He had also bought out the bar, so there would be unlimited drinks for everyone in attendance. This was definitely a night that I had once looked forward to, before the hit on the trap house. Now, no party, no VIP, no poppin' bottles could take my mind off of avenging my nigga, Rico's, death.

The look on his family's face at his funeral burned in my mind as Omari drove through the city towards Hyde Park. I couldn't shake the guilt that I felt for the tears in Rico's daughter's eyes. But none of them had shown me an ounce of anger. They hadn't made me feel the guilt that I was suffocating myself with; they had actually thanked me for helping him be such a lucrative provider for his family. But I could see the sadness in their eyes as wonder set in of how they would now provide for themselves. I vowed to never let them go hungry, though.

As we arrived at the valet, I got out of the car with a cloudy mind. A lot of our people greeted me as we walked along the sidewalk and into the Promontory. Like myself, there was some sadness in their eyes as well because, though we knew better, we were all expecting to see Fred and Rico. Luckily for us, Fred would eventually have the opportunity to party with us again. But my nigga, Rico, a nigga I'd partied with all of my life, was gone forever. I could only think about making a motherfucker pay as me, Omari, and Jasmine made our way through the crowd toward the VIP section that Geno had reserved for us.

Again, people were greeting me, but I could barely pay attention. I barely nodded my head and shook hands as I wished that I would have followed my first mind and stayed at the crib. I even wished that I had answered some of Rachel's calls and let her come over and comfort me with some slow head, anything to make this feeling go away for a little while.

I was seriously considering acting like I was going to the bathroom but actually dipping out of the nearest exit and taking an Uber to the crib. I needed to be looking for this punk ass bitch, Shug, not turning up. I had made up my mind to dip off as Eboni hugged me and said, "Hey, Capone. Thanks for coming."

Obviously, Jasmine had told her that I wasn't feeling being there.

I barely paid attention as she said, "This is my girl, Capri. We work together."

I didn't even bother to look into shorty's eyes as I shook her hand weakly and mumbled, "What up, tho?" But then her smell actually caught my attention more than anyone in the club had. Her perfume was a familiar smell that gave a nigga chills, so I found her eyes and clearly lost my cool.

It was *her.* Standing before me with slanted eyes surrounded by long lashes at the top and bottom, staring curiously into mine, I knew it was her. Though I was drunk as fuck that night at Club Liv, I didn't have to look harder or think twice; I knew it was her.

## CAPRI

*SHIT! Shit, shit, shit, shit!*

Eboni looked at the terror in my eyes and the smile on Capone's face in shock and confusion as Capone continued to hold my hand. Eboni and I hadn't known each other for that long, and we weren't even that close of friends, but I thanked God that she was, at least, cool enough to realize the tension between me and Capone and said, "And this is her *boyfriend*, Maine."

Yes, Maine had shown up at Eboni's party about ten minutes ago. He wasn't even fucking invited. I had made it clear that I was attending the party alone, but that had only made Maine's suspicions that I was leaving him for another nigga increase, so his stalking ass had shown up. I knew that he had to have stalked my Facebook page or gone through my phone to even know where the party was.

Capone wiped the smile off of his face quick as hell when he heard "boyfriend," and actually had the nerve to look at Maine like he was a problem. Maine had the audacity to put his arm around my waist, cupping his hand on the curve of my hip, as he reached out to shake Capone's hand. Then to fuck my night up further, Capone dismissed the shit out of Maine by ignoring Maine's gesture, turning his back, and telling Eboni, "Happy birthday, G. Where the bottles at?"

Again, Eboni peeped everything, so she quickly directed Capone towards the other end of VIP where an immense amount of bottles of all kinds were in a barrel. Literally, a waitress had wheeled a barrel full of ice and, at least, fifty bottles to VIP as other waitresses followed her waving sparklers in the air.

I was glad that Eboni had taken Capone away, but I was also reluctant because I knew that as soon as they were out of earshot, Maine was about to start acting like a bitch ...and that's exactly what happened.

"Where the fuck you know that nigga from?"

I sucked my teeth. "Didn't you just hear Eboni introduce me to him?"

"That don't mean shit..."

I tuned his bitch ass out. I wanted to tell him the truth so fucking bad. I wanted to be like, "Yea, I met that fine ass nigga in Miami, gave him the pussy, and have been fantasizing about him wearing this pussy out ever since!" But for the sake of not fucking up Eboni's party, I just shook my head in disgust and sat on the couch along the wall with my arms folded tightly in irritation and the straight up horniness that had taken over my body as soon as I looked into Capone's eyes.

Gawd damn, Capone was fine! Shat! It was so hard for me to keep my eyes off of him as Maine bitched into my ear.

"That's the nigga you leavin' me for, ain't it?"

*Fuck it.* "I'm leaving you because you ain't on shit. I'm leaving you because you still doin' petty shit like jackin' niggas at the age of twenty-three. I'm leaving you because I don't want to get caught up in your ignorant, petty ass bullshit that's going to get you, me or my kids killed one day."

I thought that beyond the 2 Chainz blaring through the club's sound system, he had actually heard me. Not just what I'd said, but how serious this was to me.

But he hadn't heard shit. He stared at me through his senseless brown eyes and said, "I hit a lick. I told you that. I'mma be rolling in a minute, then we straight. I told you that."

I didn't care. Yes, it seemed as if for the past few weeks Maine and his crew had more money coming in, but I knew Maine was too stupid to flip the money correctly. He would spend it all on shoes, clothes, jewelry and other stupid shit that had no value. He was running through that money like a young nigga and hadn't asked me to put up one dollar. I knew that soon, the money would run out, and he would have to steal and risk his life again.

I didn't even want to know where he got that product from because he for damn sure couldn't afford to have bought whatever he was dealing. I shook my head in repulsion as I jumped to my feet.

"Where the fuck you goin'?" I heard his ignorant, irritating voice spit at me.

I cringed and shouted over my shoulder, "Bathroom!"

# CAPONE

"Fuck is wrong with you?" Omari asked as he watched the dumbfounded look on my face curiously.

I couldn't take my eyes off of her as I told him, "That's her."

"Who?"

"*Her.* Shorty from Miami."

"Club Liv?" Omari asked as he grabbed a bottle of 1738 off the table in front of us.

I nodded, still staring at her. "Yep."

"Damn. Who's that with her? Her nigga?"

"Yea, but I don't give a fuck."

Omari cocked his head to the side and sarcastically smirked at me.

"What, motherfucker?" I asked, actually knowing exactly what he was reacting to. It was blowing me as well, but I had to be a man and play the shit off.

"You smilin'."

"No, I'm not."

"That wasn't a fucking question."

"I'm telling you, anyway." But I *was* smiling. I felt it. My face felt tight as hell as I tried my damnest not to allow the grin, fed by the joy of seeing her, to force its way through my teeth. But, fuck, I couldn't help it, so I let it free.

"Nigga!" Omari laughed.

"What?"

"You all grinnin' and shit. You ain't smiled in weeks."

He was right. But seeing her was making me remember the last time I'd been happy as fuck—Miami. I had been with Fred and Rico then, and I had met the only woman that made a nigga's heart skip a beat.

"You sprung, nigga," Omari chuckled.

"Fuck you," I laughed, not even bothering to deny it.

"What you gon' do?"

"Get her fucking number."

"Stop staring at her. Her nigga lookin' over here."

My neck snapped towards Omari. "Fuck that nigga!" The way I was feeling, I was itching to pop a motherfucka.

"For real, though. You don't know her situation. She might have to go home with that nigga."

"No, she don't."

Omari nearly dropped his drink as his eyes bucked.

"Man, stop it with the dramatics," I laughed again as I looked her way...again. Yea, her guy was staring right at me, but I couldn't help but keep my eyes on her. I had been waiting to see her for so long, and now she was right in front of me, wrapped in the smallest, yellow dress which bounced off of her black skin beautifully. Her long extensions were in a style that reminded me Kenya Moore's hair; a nigga only knew that because my guilty pleasure while smoking weed in the house alone was ratchet ass TV. There was nothing better than watching those fine ass women with big booties whoop ass on TV. The shit was hilarious, especially when you're high.

But there was nothing funny about the way Capri's thick thighs fell out of the bottom of that dress. Her skin was so smooth and shiny that I just wanted to run my tongue from her ankle and all the way up until my face disappeared under her dress. My dick was getting hard the longer I looked at her. I had never seen a creature so beautiful in my life.

I continued to stare at her, now with concern, because dude was obviously in her ear saying some fucked up shit, and she clearly wasn't happy. The look on her face told me that if I went over there and took her from that nigga, she would be more than okay with it.

A storm was brewing inside me. If this nigga didn't get out of her face, I was going to rip my gun from my waist and pop his ass. I was going to take my anger out on him. But for the first time in my life, I cared about someone more than my need to be a gangsta, so I tore my eyes away from her and gave my attention to Omari. "You right. Let me stop."

Besides, I couldn't have anybody in this VIP thinking I was less than the bad boy I was, so I couldn't let them see me softly drooling over this girl like this. I was choosing to avoid her for now, but she was *not* going to leave the party before she talked to me. That was on my life. That was on Fred and Rico.

Minutes later, I got my opportunity. I saw a weird exchange between her and ol' boy, then she stood angrily and stomped off.

As soon as I stood up, it was as if Omari was watching the exchange as well because he started cracking up as I walked away.

When I saw that that punk ass nigga was watching my every move, I stopped, turned and told Omari, "If that nigga moves an inch, kill him."

## CAPRI

Luckily, there was no line at the bathroom, so I was able to barge right in. I closed the door, took a deep breath, and looked up at the ceiling, asking God why I was being punished. I couldn't wrap my head around Maine showing up at this party and then the bad boy of my dreams showing up out of thin air like a knight in shining armor. I wanted so desperately to go out there and resume the night in Miami that had gotten interrupted, but we were no longer on vacation. This was real life. I knew that he probably thought I was a big hoe and was regretting the time he had spent with me.

As I stood with both of my hands on the sink and my head down, I heard the doorknob turning aggressively.

"Somebody's in here!"

Whoever was at the door didn't get the fucking picture because I kept hearing the doorknob turning behind my back.

"I said somebody is in here, damn!"

When I heard, "Open the door, bae," my knees got weak and my pussy embarrassingly leaked. I spun around and quickly opened the door.

Before I could take him all in, he slammed the door, locked it and then was all over me. His arms wrapped around me, and I seemed to melt into his grasp. His smell, which I remembered so well, engulfed my senses. His big hands cuffed my ass perfectly, and he took my mouth with his and kissed me so passionately that the sexual tension between us scared me. I wanted to pull up my dress and give him this pussy, especially as his fingers ran through my weave and our tongues fought seductively. But he started to pull my dress up for me, and my knees weakened at the anticipation of that dick thrusting inside of me.

But as my ass hit the cold sink, I woke up and realized what the fuck we were doing.

"Stop," I insisted as I weakly pushed him away. And that was when I was able to look into his eyes and finally take him all in. He looked so fucking good as he stood before me. He hadn't put much effort into getting dressed. He simply had on a hoodie and jeans, but that told me that he was just that damn gorgeous that he didn't need labels to give him sex appeal. Even without any labels on or any extravagant clothes, this motherfucka looked better than any man in the building.

"I'm sorry. I couldn't help it. I didn't come in here for this. But I couldn't help myself," he said, looking me up and down, licking his lips.

His eyes on me tortured the fuck out of me and made me wish that I could just have the mind frame that I did in Miami and give the man what he wanted. But now that he was here, I realized that I had the chance to actually do more than just fuck him randomly at some club. I stared at him, realizing that that was actually what I wanted to do. I wanted to get to know him, but I knew that, considering the way that we met, I didn't have that option.

"Then what did you come in here for?" I asked him, forcing his eyes on mine instead of my cleavage.

"To get your number so that I can take you away from that bitch ass nigga that you came in here with."

When he smiled cockily, I melted.

*I'm so glad I wore panties.*

"He's not really my boyfriend," I tried to explain.

He shook his head saying, "I really don't care, ma."

"No, seriously, I'm breaking up w—"

"No, ma, actually I *really* don't give a fuck. I've been thinking about you since I saw you in Miami, and as far as I'm concerned, you mine."

I cocked my head dramatically. "I'm yours?"

The way his eyes bore into mine intimidated the fuck out of me. "Yes, Capri, you *are* mine."

I was hesitant. I didn't believe him. It was unbelievable that he had actually been thinking about me when I was thinking about him.

He saw my hesitance and told me, "We kicked it so well. The pussy was good; don't get me wrong." He chuckled. "But I want to hang out again. Honestly."

I shuddered and smiled so big. I didn't care if he saw the glee on my face. "Then, I guess you should save my phone number then."

# CHAPTER 5

## MAINE

"You gotta leave town."

Shug's eyes bucked, and he started to choke on the weed in his lungs. "The fuck you mean I gotta leave town?"

I looked up at the ceiling of my aunt's crib with impatience. "Why wouldn't you have to leave town? Fred can identify you whenever he start talkin'. Take some of this work, get the fuck outta town, and make you a life somewhere else so we can continue to get this money, instead of somebody planning our funerals."

"I'm not leaving my girl, and ain't no convincing Amiyah to leave for good."

I chuckled. *This nigga can't be serious.*

"You gotta think beyond the pussy for a minute. He is alive. He will start talking. The streets are already sayin' how them niggas is lookin' for whoever hit the spot. The moment he identifies you, it's a wrap. "

Shug, obviously thinking this shit was a game, simply shrugged his shoulders. "I'm not the one that killed him."

"But they know *you*, not me."

That was fact. Shug was the one that had turned up with them on many nights. He was the one with pictures all over social media and shit like a bitch. Me? I was a low-key type of dude because I knew the bullshit I did on a regular basis. I didn't need shit like Facebook and Instagram to give me away to some niggas or the cops that were looking for me. I didn't even allow people to take pictures of me.

Shug didn't even look me in my eyes. I had been getting this attitude from him since the day we hit that spot. He was in his feelings about his friend being dead, but he had no problem flipping the bricks we had stolen. He was just as guilty since he too was making money off of the turmoil we'd caused. He and Amiyah were living a lot better now. They were no longer struggling to pay their bills. They weren't living a life of luxury, and neither was I, but we were going to get there slowly but surely. I could imagine myself riding in a Bentley by next summer, and that shit made Fred's pain and Rico's death worth it.

"I may have been the one doing the shooting, but you was there, and that's just as bad. The moment they find out who you are, you're just as much of a dead man as I am. If you leave town for a little while, shit will go a lot easier."

I could see it in his face that he still didn't agree.

Shug had heard through mutual homies that Fred was alive but unresponsive after we hit the spot. Now, he had heard that Fred was getting a little better. I knew then that we had to think fast and Shug leaving town was the only way.

We were the type of niggas that stole what we wanted: cars, drugs, money. But Capri was right. Every time I took two steps forward, I took one step back. It was as if God was punishing me for the way that I had been living my life, and that punishment was to not let me get on the way I wanted to. But things were looking promising now. The bricks we stole from that trap house were making us a weekly income that we had never seen before.

Shug and I had split the fifteen thousand dollars we'd stolen, along with the drugs. We were also making bread from selling the drugs to local crackheads until we could find a buyer for the five bricks. We hadn't made a move on selling the bricks because we had to be careful. We didn't want word getting out that somebody was trying to get off product in the area. If that happened, Omari and Capone would know that it was us that had hit their spot. For now, we could only get this product off quarter by quarter and eight ball by eight ball. It would take some time to make large amounts of money that way, but it was, at least, steady income.

I know Shug didn't want to walk away from this shit, but this was the only way for us to keep making this money and keep breathing.

He would have to get over it.

## CAPRI

After giving Capone my phone number in the bathroom at Eboni's party Friday night, he let me go untouched...thankfully. I didn't think I could take that man putting his hands on me again, especially if I had to go back and deal with Maine.

Luckily for me, Capone decided to be a gentleman and hadn't blown up my spot. He let me go back to VIP and lingered in the crowd for a while, therefore not giving us away. However, after getting back to the VIP area and seeing that Maine had that crazy ass look in his eyes, I was ready to go. It was obvious that I wasn't going to have a good time with Maine being bitchy, anyway. I told Eboni goodbye and left, but Capone had been texting me all night after the party and all day today.

I didn't know what to think of Capone. He was like a breath of fresh air. I never thought that I would see him again, and once he came into the bathroom, trying to rip my clothes off, I thought that all he would want from me was sex. But we had been conversing about everything except sex. He mostly talked about his friend, Fred, who had gotten shot about a month ago, and his friend, Rico, who had unfortunately passed away. He didn't go into the details of the shooting but was very forthcoming with not dealing with Rico's death very well. I myself had lost one of my best friends during junior year of high school, so I was able to relate.

Teresa had been, and always will be, the fourth member of me, Amiyah and Joi's crew. She was with her boyfriend when somebody had driven past and shot up his Chevy. He was the target, but she died on the scene along with him. It hurt like a motherfucka to have to bury her. Me, Amiyah and Joi weren't the same for a very long time, and sometimes we found ourselves having to find the courage to talk about Teresa without crying.

I thought that me and Capone would be talking about going out, what happened in Miami, or the fact that I had a boyfriend. Yet, we mostly talked about the things we had in common, which was losing a loved one.

Even though the conversations were somber, I was glad to have somebody to take my mind off of Maine. I had managed to convince him that it was just in his head that I knew Capone. I had also allowed him to think that he could do anything in his power to convince me to stay, while eagerly awaiting approval for an apartment that was perfect for me and the kids in Hyde Park.

I had sense enough to know that I technically was not Capone's, as he had so cockily stated in the bathroom. I wanted to relive that night in Miami so bad, but now I also looked forward to spending some time with him in my new place. I wanted to get to know the man behind the bad boy persona, tattoos, expensive clothes and luxury cars. I missed dating, Netflix and chill night, and all of the cute things that people did while they were courting. I had spent three years being a housewife with a negative dude that barely took me on real dates, so this was definitely going to be interesting.

# CAPONE

"Yes, Capone. Fuck this pussy, baby. Oh my God! Yes!"

She was throwing that ass back on my dick as if it was easy to take all these inches, but she was also hunching that back, which told me otherwise.

I smacked her ass and demanded, "Arch that back."

She did as I told her to, then I grabbed her waist with both hands and decided to get this shit over with. I needed to buss this nut bad as hell. It had been building up inside of me since I was in the bathroom with Capri at the Promontory last night. I couldn't believe I had did that to that girl. I went to the bathroom with only the intention of getting her phone number, but as soon as she opened the bathroom door, memories of Miami hit me like a ton of bricks, and I just had to relive that moment. I was glad that she was a good girl and pushed me off of her, because oddly, I didn't want things between us to be just about sex. For some reason, I wanted to get to know shorty and see what she was about so that maybe we could do things beyond just fucking.

I chuckled to myself as I realized that I was even thinking beyond fucking.

Rachel deserved this dick that I was giving her. She had been by my side as much as she could, even taking off work to make sure that I was okay when the robbery first happened. She deserved this dick, but I wanted nothing more than to give it to Capri. I was actually considering giving it to her long-term, not just for a few random nights and then we lost touch because we really didn't know each other. I didn't know what it was about her that was even making me feel this way; I guess it was that connection shit that Jasmine and Omari, and Eboni and Geno had told me about so many times.

"Arrrgh! Fuck!" My nut was coming down, so I closed my eyes and imagined that I was releasing it into Capri, instead of the phat ass of a chick that I really didn't even want to be in, into a condom that separated us from really being intimate with each other.

After cumming, I held onto her waist as I slipped out of her, holding the top of the condom as I pulled out. I could see the longing in Rachel's eyes as, instead of lying beside her and spooning with her, I sat on the edge of the bed. I knew better than to lay down to get comfortable. Even though she had a nice condo in Bronzeville that a nigga could comfortably chill at, I knew what she wanted from me, and I had no interest in giving her that, so I stood up to leave. I heard her inhale sharply, so I knew some bullshit was coming. Luckily, my cell phone rang, but unluckily... my cell phone rang. Ever since I had gotten that devastating call about Fred and Rico, I cringed whenever my phone rang late at night.

I was visibly relieved when I looked at the display and saw that it was Carlos.

"What up though?" I answered. "You back?"

"Just touched down," Carlos replied.

I looked at Rachel to give her a silent goodbye, but she was ignoring me by looking up at the ceiling. I shrugged my shoulders, kissed her forehead anyway, and made my way out of her bedroom. I wasn't going to kiss her ass. We didn't have the connection necessary to have the relationship she wanted. I didn't even know what a connection meant until I met Capri. Our conversations since yesterday had only proven that you couldn't force a connection with someone you didn't feel it with. It just happened...like it was automatically happening with Capri. I felt bad for that because Rachel was a good girl, but I would rather know that I didn't want her now, than six years, two kids, and a dog from now.

"Good shit," I told Carlos as I left Rachel's condo, locking the bottom lock behind myself.

Carlos was the most hustling Puerto Rican I'd ever known. He was in the ranks with Fred in our organization, and I needed him to take Fred's place until Fred got better. Omari and I had a new crib to open a new spot in. We had just replaced the drugs that were stolen with a run that Rico went on for us to California. Now, it was time to get back to the regularly scheduled program while the hunt for Shug continued.

"Any word on this nigga Shug yet?"

"We tryin' to find out where he stay now. Of course, he shut down all of his social media pages. I heard that his mother stays in the Manor. You want us to hit her?"

I chuckled, saying, "Down boy. Nah, dawg. We ain't gon' stoop that low."

Our organization didn't run like that. We wasn't like these young thugs in Chicago killing innocent bystanders and shooting every other day. We only came at those that came at us, and that was rare, far and in between. Even though it hurt my soul that these goofy niggas took away a good man and damn near took the life of another one, I wasn't going to allow anybody else to reap their punishment but them.

"But we definitely gon' get these motherfuckas," I swore to Carlos. "I put that on my life. That's my word."

# CHAPTER 6

## CAPRI

♫ *All of my hoes is exotic*
*None of your hoes is invited*
*All of my hoes is exotic*
*None of your hoes is invited*
*All of my hoes is exotic*
*None of your hoes is invited* ♫

I was having one of the best days of my life. I was in a good fucking mood. Not only had I been talking to Capone nonstop for the last three days, but we were also going out tonight for the first time. I was in my room dancing around, happy as hell, and doing my hair because I was supposed to meet up with him in an hour. You couldn't tell me that the sun wasn't shining, even though there was a light drizzle outside.

I was so ready to see Capone. It was crazy how him being in my life had made me feel so much better about everything, even Maine, who I seemed to forget about day by day. Capone had never even brought Maine's name up. I knew that I needed to tell Capone, but I wanted to wait until we were face-to-face to explain my relationship situation. To make Capone accept the fact that I was living with another man even easier, I was wearing the tightest, hunter green tube top dress that made me look stacked, with the help of a pair of Spanx that was holding a bitch's stomach *in*, smoothing my lumps and bumps. With a pair of cream suede booties that were peep toe, my ass stood up like a stallion. My hair was slicked back into a ponytail, and my face had a light beat.

I was in great spirits as I danced around to the trap music that was playing out of the iPod dock on the dresser. You couldn't tell me shit. I was *living*... until the bedroom door burst open. I thought it was one of the kids, who I was going to drop off at my Auntie Dawn's house. I wanted to hang out peacefully without Maine calling me every five minutes asking me when I was coming home because he was watching them. And luckily my mother had gone missing again, so it was safe for the kids to be with my aunt.

But instead of seeing one of the kids, I turned around and saw an aggravated and angry Maine.

When I saw his face, I didn't bother to hide my disappointment that it was him, turned back to the mirror, and continued to apply my lipstick.

"You goin' to see your other nigga?"

I asked with an aggravated sigh, "What the hell are you talking about, Maine?"

I heard him grumble, "You think you slick as hell."

"I don't need to hear this shit. Don't ruin my day because you have a fucking attitude that I have nothing to do with."

"You have everything to do with my attitude. I know you on some bullshit, Capri. "

I rolled my eyes into the back of my head. He didn't know shit. Ever since I had been talking to Capone, I had been keeping my phone by my side. Hell, I even slid it under my pillow when I was asleep.

"I'm sick of you playing me like I'm some sort of bitch ass nigga!"

Nothing could fuck with my mood today, especially not Maine's punk ass attitude. So I kept applying my lipstick in the mirror and moving my hips to the music. I knew that it was pissing him off, but I would have never thought that he would have run up on me. He grabbed me by my shoulder so rough that I shrieked out in pain. He then spun me around and slammed my back against the dresser so hard that it actually sent a sharp pain charging up my spine.

Instead of being scared, I got heated. "Get your fuckin—"

*Phwap!*

He smacked the shit out of me! There was so much rage in him. He wouldn't let me go. He kept standing there with his hands tightly on my shoulders and his nails digging into my skin as my eyes bulged out of my head in disbelief. No matter how much me and Maine had argued, fussed and fought, we had never physically fought. He had never put his hands on me, so my usual bite was muffled by complete and utter shock. I couldn't believe that his bitch ass had the balls to hit me, but wasn't man enough to do something with his fucking life.

As I wrestled to get out of his grasp, he spat, "I know you been playin' me!"

I fought like hell to get away from him so that I could put my hands on him, but then one of the kids burst into the room.

"Mommy, what's wrong? I heard you screa—" Nikki stopped in her tracks once she saw Maine angrily all over me.

"Let me go," I growled lowly as I yanked my way out of his grasp. And he let me, knowing that he would dig himself into a deeper hole by fighting me in front of the kids.

I prayed that he wouldn't chase me, that he would stop before Nicholas came into the room next. They had seen enough bullshit in their short lives. They didn't need to see anymore.

I snatched my keys and purse from the bed as I told Nikki, "Let's go, baby."

As I barged out of the room, Maine followed closely behind us, continuing to shoot threats and accusations at me.

"I know you fuckin' around on me—"

"Not in front of the kids!" I warned.

"Fuck that shit!" he barked.

I couldn't believe that Maine was so upset that he would do this in front of the kids. He knew how I felt about this. He knew how I protected them. He was obviously so pissed that he was at the point that he actually believed what he was saying. I couldn't imagine why he all of a sudden was going off like this, but I had to get me and the kids the fuck out of there. It was one thing for me to deal with his ignorance, irresponsibility, and inability to be a man. But what I was definitely not about to deal with was him having the audacity to put his broke ass hands on me!

"Nicholas!" I shouted, ignoring the feeling of Maine's hot breath on the back of my neck.

"When I find out who that nigga is, I'm killin' him!" he seethed.

Nicholas was sitting wide-eyed on the floor in front of the television. I hurriedly picked him up, grabbed Nikki's hand and rushed towards the door with Maine still on our heels. However, once I got to the front door and snatched it open, I knew that he was too much of a punk to follow me outside. He was more concerned about how he looked to the hood and maintaining his fraud ass reputation of being "that nigga." So as I ran out of the door with the kids, he didn't follow. He just stood in the doorway, and as I put the kids into their car seats, I could see him glaring a hole into my back.

After buckling them in, I hurried around to the driver's side door while getting my cell phone out of my purse. I hopped in, quickly closed the door, and turned the ignition while dialing Amiyah's phone number.

"I was *just* about to call you," she answered as I headed out of the driveway.

"I need a favor," I hurriedly spoke. "Maine just spazzed out on me and smacked the shit out of me." My eyes were burning as I fought the urge to burst into tears in front of the kids.

"He did what?!"

But Amiyah's reaction was making it hard not to cry over the realization of how fucked up this shit was. "Can you watch the kids for me while I figure out where the fuck we're going to live?" My voice cracked. "I'm not going back home. Fuck that."

"You can go home. Kick his ass out!"

"I'm not fighting with Maine no more, Amiyah. I'm done."

She sighed, saying, "I feel you. I can't watch them for you, though. I was calling to tell you that me and Shug are on our way out of town."

"Out of town? Where are you going?"

"He jumped up this morning saying that he wanted to see his mother, so we're going to St Louis."

I sighed, frustrated that she was leaving me at a time like this and that I was going to have to call Joi to ask her. She didn't have kids and was an only child. Her patience for children was thin, so I wasn't comfortable leaving them with her.

"Let me call you back," I told Amiyah.

I hung up before she even agreed and dialed Joi, attempting to drive, calm down and make calls all at the same damn time. However, calling Joi was useless. She didn't even answer the phone.

I cringed as I approached a red light, realizing that I had to call my Aunt Dawn. I didn't want the kids around my mother for long periods of time, but I was going to have to bite the bullet for a while until I figured something out. I didn't know where I was going to end up sleeping for the next few days, and I didn't want the kids on somebody's couch with me. Me staying with my Aunt Dawn was still not an option; I would not be comfortable sleeping with my purse under my head in order to make sure that my mother wasn't robbing me blind.

# CAPONE

My cell rang, and when I looked over in the passenger seat and saw that it was Capri's name on the display screen, I actually smiled. I actually fucking smiled. Just knowing that this girl was calling me put a smile on my face, and I felt so soft. But I swallowed my pride and accepted the fact that I was happy that she was calling me and that I was about to see her soon.

"What's up, pretty lady?" I answered.

I was immediately on guard when she sighed deeply in response, instead of those sexy ass feminine giggles that she usually responded with.

I immediately slowed down and pulled over to the curb on Stony Island. I had just left the new trap house that we were setting up. I had taken care of business all day and was ready to kick it with my black beauty, but it didn't sound like that was about to happen.

I gripped the steering wheel tightly as I regretfully asked her, "What's wrong?"

She sighed again before saying, "I can't see you tonight. It's been a fucked up d—"

"Here's your key, ma'am," someone in the background interrupted her.

"Are you at a hotel?" I asked her.

She slowly answered, "Yeeeah... Well, a motel."

"Why?"

This time her sigh was matched with a groan. "I...uh... finally broke up with my boyfriend. I left the house. I didn't have anywhere else to go, so I'm at a motel."

"Which one?"

"This motel off of Sibley."

"I know it. I'm on my way. Text me your room number."

I hung up before she could fight that I was coming despite the night she was having. No matter what, I was going to see her tonight. I had waited long enough to see her, and I wasn't going to let that bitch ass nigga keep me from it.

****

Once I got to the room, it was hard for me to focus on the problem at hand... because I was having a problem in my Rock Revival jeans. Even though she was obviously upset, I couldn't help but appreciate her curves in that dress. I was a slim fit type of dude. I wasn't as wide and cocky as Omari, but even though I was a slightly smaller build, my body was large and hard. I could easily pick a nigga up and slam his ass as easily as I could pick up a woman of two-hundred pounds and wrap her thick thighs around my legs. As I sat in a chair and watched Capri, I imagined myself doing just that to her again, but I had to be cool, take care of her emotionally and let her know that the physical was not all that I wanted from her.

"So, what happened? You wanna talk about it?"

She ran her hand over her head and smoothed out her ponytail as she shook her head. Even though I wanted to know what had happened, I especially wanted to know if that pussy nigga had done anything to harm her, but I was cool with not speaking about him. I hadn't done so since the day I had seen her at Eboni's birthday party, and I intended to keep it that way until it was necessary. I didn't want to think about her with another nigga. Any other woman that I messed with,

I imagined them fucking other niggas with not a care in the world. But not her. Not Capri.

I knew that it really wasn't my place to ask about her man until she was officially mine, and that hadn't happened yet because I wasn't trying to force anything between us. Even though I felt more for her than I did for anybody else I had ever met, I still wanted to take this slow and figure it out for my own sake. I had never experienced anything like this before, so I was being cautious as hell while enjoying her presence.

She sat on the bed and looked at me with a pout that was actually just as cute as she was. "I'm so sorry. I fucked up our first date."

"You didn't fuck anything up. I just wanted to spend time with you. As long as I can still do that, I'm good."

She looked at me as if I was unbelievable. Shit, I was unbelievable to myself. But it was how I felt around her, and I didn't feel like it was necessary to fake like I didn't. In her presence, I felt like I could let the gangsta go and just chill for once in my life. I felt safe. I was usually the one protecting people, but *she* made *me* feel safe.

"Are you okay?" she asked as she stared at me.

I looked at her as if I should be asking her that, but if she wanted to change the subject, I was going to let her do it.

I was at the point that I was willing to do whatever she wanted if it made her happy. I actually *wanted* to make her happy, and that blew the shit out of me to the point that I was holding back a smile.

I sat in a chair, legs wide, leaned back and shrugging nonchalantly. "I'm straight."

She sighed so hard that her shoulders sank. "You're lying. You still miss them."

I closed my eyes and sighed, admitting the truth. "Hell yea."

She motioned for me to sit beside her. I was hesitant at first because I was doing the best that I could to show her that I wasn't just there to get my dick wet. If I sat beside her on the bed, with her in that dress and those pretty eyes looking at me the way that she was, I didn't know how long I was going to be able to contain myself.

Despite all of that, I stood slowly and walked over to the bed, ignoring the way that her curves enticed the fuck outta me. Something told me that containing myself would be well worth it in the end.

We sat on the bed, and she let me talk about Fred and Rico until we ended up lying back on the bed and getting comfortable. We both kicked off our shoes and stared at the ceiling while I told her about all the good memories I had of Fred and Rico until we fell asleep.

# OMARI

"I can't lose you, Omari. I'll die."

I sighed, never taking my eyes off of Fred's unconscious body, but I did hold Jasmine's hand tighter.

"You're not going to lose me," I told her.

"What if that had been you in that trap house that night?"

I knew it was a bad idea to let Jasmine see Fred in this condition, but she insisted on coming with me every time I visited the hospital. The moment we started to love each other, I was open with her about the organization that Capone and I headed. She wasn't stupid. When we met, she knew that I sold drugs, but I made sure that she knew on what level I did so that when she agreed to be my wife, she was doing it with full knowledge of the nigga she would be saying "I do" to. She took that information and agreed to be my backbone in our relationship and in my business. So, when it came to shit like this, she was right there with me.

"I would never be in a trap house." Then I chuckled to lighten her mood. When she didn't laugh, I turned to look in her eyes. I saw concern flooding her eyes, and my heart went out to her. I had felt the pain of losing a lover, so I felt a lot of guilt for even putting that fear in her.

"I'm serious, Omari. We are getting married on Christmas in Jamaica so that we can live happily ever after, and that is what the fuck is going to happen. I want to live the rest of my life being your wife, not your widow."

I kissed her forehead, telling her, "You know what I've been through, and I love you, so I spend every minute of every day making sure that I never put you through the same."

"But you all are going to retaliate, right? I know you and Capone, so I know you all aren't going to let them get away with this."

I had to be honest. "Nah, we're not."

"Then they are going to retaliate for the same."

I shook my head, confidently saying, "Once we retaliate, it's over. No one will come back at us because there won't be anyone left."

# CHAPTER 7

## CAPRI

I couldn't believe that talking about old memories of deceased friends would make such a nice night.

As we talked last night, I forced myself to ignore what had happened between me and Maine. I knew better than to tell Capone about Maine slapping me. Even though I didn't know Capone that well, I was convinced that the man that I had learned about for the past couple of days was not one that would have taken a man slapping the shit out of me lightly. I *knew* that. I couldn't stand the man, but I didn't want Maine dead, and that's exactly what would happen if I told Capone the truth. So as the night went on, and Capone finally asked what happened, I simply told him that I was leaving a three-year relationship because Maine was not the man I'd thought he would be, nor the man that I needed for me and my kids. He simply nodded in response, but I could see the happiness in the back of his eyes as he learned that I was definitely a single girl. There was also remnants of uncertainty in his eyes; it was as if he knew that something more had happened than me simply leaving.

But he dropped the subject, and we continued to talk about Teresa, Fred and Rico all night, until we fell asleep. It felt so good to wake up with his arms around me. I woke up with a smile on my face, despite the stinging feeling on the left side of my face as a result of the fierce slap Maine had landed on it. Despite the disbelief of what had gone down at my house before I left last night, I rolled over and looked at a man that I felt really blessed to have in my life. He hadn't been anything to me but good conversation and presence, but that had been enough to change my life from chaos to calm. It was as if he had come in the nick of time, when God knew that everyone close to me would suddenly disappear.

As I stared at the definition of his body that I could clearly see although he was clothed in Rock Revival from head to toe, his deep voice pierced the air and scared the shit out of me. "You want breakfast?"

I chuckled from embarrassment. "How did you know that I was awake?"

His head turned toward me. When his eyes opened, and his smile appeared, my embarrassment was replaced with lust... a lot of it... tons of fucking lust... pussy just *wet!*

"You stopped snoring," he said with his smile that teased the fuck outta me.

I fought hard not to lick my lips.

My mouth dropped as I slapped him playfully. "I do not snore."

"You was last night."

I pouted, saying, "I had a bad day yesterday. I was really tired."

He reached over and lightly pinched my stomach. "I know. I'm not judging."

His eyes dug into mine and, suddenly, I was at a loss for words, and so was he. Fuck, there was so much gawd damn tension between us, sexual tension that wanted to relive the night we first met so badly.

I wanted him terribly. It was obvious that he was trying to treat me like a lady, but I didn't want to be treated like a fucking lady. I wanted him to rip that fucking dress off of me, get his bad boy ass on top of me, and punish this pussy as he had done in Miami. I knew he could see it in my eyes. I knew he could probably smell my sexual tension as it dripped out of my pussy. I could tell by the way that he looked at me that he knew exactly what I wanted.

He started to come close to me as if my wishes were going to be his command. I hated the fact that I was hyperventilating as he came closer and closer to me. His lips were inches away from mine, and I anticipated him sucking my lips right before I sucked that dick, which I had imagined in my mouth for weeks after we met.

He kissed my forehead so softly that I was able to enjoy the feeling of his lips on my skin again after months of anticipation and wishful thinking. I knew that it was about to go down. Finally, I was about to get that dick again. Even if he never talked to me again after this day, I didn't give a fuck. Even if it turned into just sex and the conversations stopped, I wanted that dick.

But instead of getting that dick, I got, "Let's go get some breakfast, babe."

Though I smiled on the outside and said, "Okay," I was cringing and screaming on the inside, *Damn!*

**\*\*\*\***

I laughed so hard that I almost choked on my sausage. "Why are you looking at me like that?"

"Because I don't believe you."

"It's true; I swear."

Capone's eyebrow rose as he gave me this sexy ass smirk from across the table. "For real?"

*"For real,"* I insisted. "I have not had sex since you and I did it in Miami."

"Yo' nigga wasn't fuckin' you?" he asked unbelievably.

*"I* wasn't fucking *him."*

Behind the pulsating feeling between my legs that Capone was constantly causing as he stared into my eyes while he demolished a skillet, guilt crept back into my heart. The pregnancy that I had terminated came back to mind. I had totally convinced myself that the baby was Maine's. Convincing myself that it was Maine's made the guilt tolerable, even though there was a chance that it could have been Capone's. But even after Capone and I met again, and we talked about that night at Club Liv, neither one of us remembered whether he had on a condom or not. So, I tried to ignore the immense amount of guilt and just put the whole thing in the back of my mind. It was something that would just go to the grave with me, but it was also something that I would never do again.

"After getting this dick, you just couldn't let that nigga touch you again, huh?" Capone asked, boastful.

I smiled. "You got that right, Daddy."

For once, it seemed as though I had taken his breath away. At the sound of "Daddy," he hesitated a bit, and it looked as if he had to catch his breath.

"You better stop playing with me, girl," he told me cockily.

I smiled devilishly, my legs bouncing uncontrollably under the table. *Damn, this nigga is fine.*

"What's your name? Your real name," I asked.

I had never asked, and I needed to know him; the real him.

"Terrell Morris. You?"

"Neisha Cobb."

He smiled, nodded and raised his glass. "Nice to meet you."

I giggled and returned the gesture. "Nice to meet you too."

# MAINE

I had been selling the drugs that I stole from DBD out of my aunt's house on the west side, so that's where I had been since Capri and the kids left the house. I couldn't stand going home. It made me realize even more that I hadn't accomplished being the man that Capri wanted and needed.

I was finally more comfortable now that Shug had left town. Everything was supposed to be perfect now, but it wasn't. I was feeling like the man, but now, I didn't have the family that I was supposed to be a man for. I couldn't believe that I had spazzed out so bad that I put my hands on Capri, but the shit was freaking me out that she was actually stepping out on me. I had heard everything she had said about me being more responsible and being a real nigga, even though I tried to act like she didn't know what the fuck she was talking about. Now, I was making some cash, being a real man, and she was with somebody else. That felt like a smack in my face, so I smacked her so that she would feel the same pain physically that I was emotionally.

For years, I had taken advantage of the fact that she would never leave, but she really had this time. Now, there was nothing I could do to get her back because I had done the unthinkable. She wouldn't even answer my calls. I had been blowing her phone up all night and sending her text messages, but I could tell that she had put me on her block list.

I had done a lot to please that girl. One nigga was dead, one was clinging to life, and my dude, Shug, couldn't even hit his own streets; all because I was trying to come up for her. So, I wasn't about to let her leave me after all of that, especially for another nigga.

## CAPONE

*Urgh, what the fuck am I doin'?* I thought as I walked up to Adriana's front door. Adriana was the last person that I felt like dealing with after the good time I had been having with Capri. I wanted to be with her, not Adriana, but I had to give her space if I didn't want to fall hard and fast for her. But I had had a hard dick since the moment I laid in that bed with Capri. If I wanted to continue to get to know her without sex being involved, I needed to get this nut off, and not off in one of my hands.

Rachel was for sure offering a nigga the pussy, but I was so tired of her looking at me like she was waiting for me to ask for her hand in marriage that I didn't feel like faking the funk with her tonight. Alicia hadn't answered the phone, so I hit up Adriana. She was a freak that gave some great, sloppy head and squirted. She fucked with me from time to time, when her husband was out of town, which was often because he drove trucks. Luckily, he was gone tonight.

I shook thoughts of Capri out of my head and went ahead and knocked on the door with a heart full of reluctance... until the door opened and this five-foot-nine, chocolate, slim-thick chick dressed in nothing but a thong and heels was standing on the other side. Her body was straight off of the stage of King of Diamonds in Miami. Capri had hardened my dick, but now it was pulsating.

"Damn," I mumbled.

Her smile was wicked but lovely as she literally purred, "C'mon in."

"Yea, come on in, bad boy," I heard Adriana's voice purr behind her. "I know you aren't being shy."

The chocolate chick stepped to the side, and Alicia appeared behind her, dressed identical to her, except her redbone body didn't have on the thong, only heels.

I cocked my head to the side and shook it in amazement. Adriana never ceased to amaze me. The lengths she went to show me that she would do anything to please this dick was amazing. Usually, whenever she brought another chick to our escapades, she told me first. This move she had just pulled tonight was a shocker but was definitely what I needed. Thanks to Capri, I had enough nut built up inside of me for the both of these chicks.

# CHAPTER 8

## CAPRI

As soon as my shift ended at eleven p.m. the next day, I was running out of that damn hospital. I was so tired from hanging out with Capone for the last two days that I was craving for that hotel bed. I didn't give a damn if it was a Saturday night.

After breakfast, Capone and I had hung out all day. I just rode around with him as he took care of business, but I still had a good time just being in his presence. He seemed like he was really enjoying being in mine as well. It also turned me on even more that he was the type of man that took care of his shit. Unlike Maine, who waited on me to pay bills and make moves, Capone was taking care of his own business and making major moves all day. That made me admire and crave him even more. . He was the man's man that I had wanted Maine to be.

After running errands until late last night, he took me to dinner at a cool spot called, Mr. Brown's Lounge. We feasted on the best Jamaican food I'd had in a long time and rocked to dancehall music all night. Once our night was over and he followed me into my motel room, once again, I just knew that I was going to get the dick, but by the time I got out of the shower, he was asleep.

Then, I had gotten up early this morning to head over to my aunt's house to take the kids to school, so Capone and I finally parted ways. Once back at my motel room, I still wasn't able to go back to sleep and get some rest before my shift started at 3PM because Capone wanted to talk on Facetime all afternoon.

I was literally running across the courtyard while calling Amiyah back. I had missed her call during my shift, and I was anxious to see what was going on. It had been three days since she left, and I was ready for my girl to come back to the crib. I needed a girl's night bad. I needed to vent about Maine and brag about Capone, and Joi was still too stuck in her own world to give a fuck about what was going on in mine. Though I had been reaching out to her to vent about Maine and finding a place to live, with no response from her, the bitch had the nerve to send me a text message asking me to meet her at The Black Cat Lounge after work.

*Self-absorbed bitch.*

Fuck Joi. She was intolerable without Amiyah being around. I was really looking forward to my girl coming home, but once Amiyah answered the phone, I learned that maybe she wasn't coming back at all.

"Hey, girl," I heard Amiyah sigh.

"What's going on? What's wrong with you?"

"Shug is trippin'. I thought this was going to be an overnight trip or something, but this nigga is getting comfortable and shit."

"What you mean?"

"Talking about his brother got a job for him here, and its more money than what he was making with Maine."

"Well, shit, ain't nothing wrong with that."

She sighed into the phone and agreed, "I know, but I miss you."

"I miss you too. I have some tea to spill."

As I made my way east on the Bishop Ford expressway, I told her about all of the voicemails and text messages that Maine had been leaving me. The side of me that had been committed to him for three years actually wanted to have some type of conversation with him about what had happened. I had never wanted to just walk out on him the way that I did. Because of the relationship that we had and his relationship with the kids, he deserved more than for me to just completely cut him off. But him getting physical with me had left me no choice.

I would have to talk to him at some point, but I was tired of the empty promises. I didn't want to hear him beg, and even though I was confident that I was never going back to him, I respected our history too much to hurt him by telling him that I would never be with him again.

"I still can't believe he hit me. It's like he's totally convinced that I'm leaving him for some other nigga, when that's not the case at all. I was ready to leave his ass before Capone ever came in the picture."

"Wait... so Capone is *in the picture?*"

A smile spread across my face as I thought of him.

I told her all about the time we spent that night in the hotel, the next day at breakfast and all day yesterday. By the time that I was done fantasizing about him, and Amiyah was done praising him, I was pulling into a parking space in front of the motel that I had been staying in.

"Girl, I can't wait to get the hell out of this motel."

Amiyah sucked her teeth. "Why? Shit, ain't it fun having somebody clean up after you?"

I giggled as I got my key card out. "Yea, but I miss my babies. And this ain't no five-star hotel."

"How is the apartment hunting going?"

"I haven't heard back from the place that I wanted. I think it's my credit, girl. I let Maine fuck my shit up, and now I can't get approved to get a fucking bag of weed on credit."

She laughed, saying, "Damn. These niggas, girl. They will suck you the fuck dry."

I laughed as well as I walked into my "home" and closed the door. I kicked off my shoes and started to disrobe as I listened to Amiyah talk shit about how Shug and Maine had fucked up everything while supposedly loving us. Our relationships weren't all bad, but shit, they could have definitely used way more good.

A knock at the door startled me just as I was done to my bra and panties, ready to get off the phone with Amiyah and hop in the shower.

"Hold on," I told her as I looked through the peephole. Seeing who it was, I groaned and uttered, "SHIT!"

"What? What's wrong?" Amiyah asked hurriedly.

Just as I whispered, "Maine is at the door," he started beating on it.

"Oh my God," I groaned.

"Don't let him in."

"I gotta open the door. He's not going to leave, and I don't feel like dealing with the fucking police tonight." Then I sighed. "Let me call you back."

"Don't let that nigga put his hands on you again."

"Girl, if he does, it's going to be a knockdown drag out in this bitch. I doubt he will, though. He feels so guilty about doing it in the first place. I'll definitely call you back—"

"Wait," she said hurriedly. "Don't tell Maine where we are."

I was turning the door knob to open it, but stopped and asked, "Why?"

"I heard Shug tell him that we were in Houston. He lied to him for a reason. I don't know why, but it must be a good reason if he's lying to his best fr—"

"I know you're in there! Open the door! I j—I just wanna talk to you, baby."

"Fuck, he's drunk," I realized. "Let me call you back."

"Okay. Don't forget what I said," she spat hurriedly before I hung up and opened the door.

Maine looked me up and down longingly for a second. He then switched back to the jealous and immature person that he had been for the past couple of weeks; he looked behind me and into the room with a glare.

"Nobody is here, Maine," I told him as he made his way inside. I asked as I closed the door. "How did you know I was here?"

"I followed you from work," he said with a shrug like it was nothing as he forced his way into the room. As he walked by me, I could smell the Remy coming out of his pores and on his breath.

*Yes, this fool is definitely drunk. Great.*

"I'm sorry for hitting you, babe," he slurred.

I just stood in front of him with my arms folded as he plopped down on the bed. His text message notification went off, but he ignored it, reached out for my hand, and brought me towards the bed. Seeing him in this vulnerable state reminded me of the old days when we would get drunk, laugh at things that weren't funny, and fuck until the sun came up. That was fun; it was happiness. It was what we didn't have anymore, and that really made me sad.

"Don't leave me for this nigga..." His voice trailed off as he lay back on the bed and brought me with him. "I'm gettin' back on. My attitude will change. I swear, baby. I'mma be able to take care of you and the kids, I promise."

His phone went off again, but he continued to ramble, ignoring it again. He was too drunk, so there was no use in saying a word; my words would go through one incoherent ear and out of the other. I just let him make all of the empty promises in the world, telling myself that I would let him sleep off the liquor and then peacefully get rid of him in the morning when I had to leave out to take the kids to school.

My thoughts made even more sense as he soon went from begging to snoring. I slipped out of his arms, out of the bed, and stood over him, staring and wondering why I couldn't just stay in the same frame of mind I had been in years ago that had me totally and utterly in love with his hood ass. I missed that shit, but I appreciated who I had matured into—the woman who knew the difference between a bum like Maine and a man like Capone. And even though Capone was not a guarantee to be the next man to make me fall stupidly in love with him, I was, at least, happy that I had grown into falling for men like him, instead of men like the one unconscious on my bed.

As I went through my bag, in order to get my loofa sponge and body wash, I could hear Maine's phone going off again. I peered at Maine, and he was still out like a light. I fought the typical female in my brain that wanted to look at that phone. I had only done it a few times during our relationship. I rarely found anything, mostly females wanting to be with the man that put on for them like he was the shit. If he ever cheated on me, he was meticulous in covering his tracks because I never found anything, so I eventually stopped looking.

However, I couldn't help but wonder. He had been constantly accusing me of being with another man. It was now nearly one in the morning, so I wondered who it was blowing him up. Even if it was a woman, I wanted to wish the bitch my blessings, thank her, and even make her and Maine some fucking pancakes in the morning.

Slipping into his pocket to get his phone was easy. He didn't wake up or move a muscle as I slid his iPhone out. I had memorized his lock code months ago, leaning on his shoulder, pretending like I was really paying attention to Scandal.

Even though it didn't seem like he would wake up 'til Sunday, I moved through the phone quickly because I was ready to get in the shower and go to sleep. I quickly scrolled his call log, saw nothing of interest and then went into his text messages. There was nothing of much interest there either, until I scrolled down and recognized a phone number.

*708-955-4464: Come hang out with me.*
*Maine: Nah. I'm good, shorty.*

*708-955-4464: I don't know why you keep acting like you don't want me. She don't want you. She's moved on. She got a new nigga, I heard.*

**Maine:** *Fuck you.*

*708-955-4464: That's what I'm trying to get you to do.*

*708-955-4464: Y'all broke up now, so what's good.*

*708-955-4464: Hellooooo?*

The number wasn't saved, but I knew exactly who the fuck it was. The realization made my heart beat like a beast inside of my chest. My head started to spin, and my fingers started to shake as I held the phone and kept scrolling through the conversation. There were so many messages that pissed me the fuck off, but specific ones had me throwing on my clothes as I continued to scroll through the conversation.

*A week ago:*

*708-955-4464: I wanna fuck you.*

**Maine:** *Lol. Oh really? I told you what I was on.*

*708-955-4464: She fuckin' with somebody else, so you can too. Fuck it.*

**Maine:** *Fuckin' with somebody else?*

*708-955-4464: Yea, I'm her best friend, I would know.*

*Three weeks ago:*

**708-955-4464:** *What you doin'?*

**Maine:** *Minding my business.*

**708-955-4464:** *Wanna mind mine?*

**Maine:** *I'm good.*

**708-955-4464:** *Thought you wanted this pussy....*

**Maine:** *I changed my mind. I want my girl.*

**708-955-4464:** *Well, she don't want you.*

*Seven weeks ago:*

**Maine:** *Capri won't pick up. You talked to her?*

**708-955-4464:** *We're leaving the clinic.*

**Maine:** *Huh? You got knocked?*

**708-955-4464:** *Nah. Your girl did.*

**Maine:** *You a gawd damn lie.*

**708-955-4464:** *Yea okay.*

**Maine:** *What's up with you, tho?*

**708-955-4464:** *What you mean?*

**Maine:** *You know exactly what I mean.*

**708-955-4464:** *What you want to be up with me?*

**Maine:** *You ain't 'bout that life.*

**708-955-4464:** *Come find out.*

I was done reading after that, and I was also done getting dressed. I took a couple of screenshots of the text messages and sent them to myself. Then my eyes fell on Maine and the gun he always kept on his side. My body flew towards him faster than I thought it would. I wasn't going for the gun, though every fiber of my being wanted to snatch it from his waist and put two holes in his head. I was putting his phone back, but then I decided against it.

*Fuck this phone*, I thought as I marched out of the room with my keys and his phone in my hand. As soon I was outside, I lunged his phone, and it shattered into a million pieces against the concrete.

I didn't even make sure that the room door was closed. I hoped that some hype broke into that room and killed his ass while I was on my way to kill somebody else.

I was on my way to the Black Cat Lounge.

# CHAPTER 9

## CAPRI

The Black Cat Lounge was a twenty-minute ride from the motel, but I got there in fifteen. I was heated, and that was to say the fucking least. This bitch, Joi, had a lot of fucking nerve trying to take my nigga from me. Granted, no, I didn't want his bum ass, but the bitch was so thirsty to have a man that she was gon' try to take mine? Nope, not goin'!

At this point, it was after one in the morning. For a Saturday night/early Sunday morning, the popular bar on 115th Street was crackin'. Despite this, I spotted Joi's ride parked near the back. I quickly parked a few spots down and hopped out, rage boiling over in me.

Security looked me up and down as I stormed towards the door. I knew that they were eyeing my appearance. I had been to this spot many times with Joi and Amiyah, so he knew

131

my usual look. Therefore, the wrinkled t-shirt, jeans, unkempt hair and bare face was throwing him off. Yet, he must have already seen Joi in the spot because he spoke to me and let me in without even checking my ID. I gave him a half-smile, knowing that he was about to be pissed at me in just a few minutes.

As soon as I saw the hoe, it was a crackin'. This bitch had been putting up a front for months. Attempting to fuck my nigga was one thing, but throwing me under the bus with both lies and truth while doing so was something completely different and worth an ass whooping on a whole 'nother level.

I spotted Joi by the bar in some nigga's face that I recognized: Reggie, the same nigga that she was pouting about the day I had gotten the abortion. I guess since Maine wasn't goin' tonight, Reggie was her next choice.

"This bitch want her nigga and everybody else's," I seethed under my breath as I pushed my way through the crowd towards her. I got a couple of fucked up comments from bitches that I pushed on my way towards my target, but I gave them a look that dared them to fuck with me, and they quickly stood down.

Joi caught my eye as I marched towards her. The bitch had the nerve to smile, though confusion with my presence was evident behind it.

As soon as I was within arm's reach of this hoe, I smacked that drink out of her hand so hard that the glass broke on contact, and flying fragments of glass split her lip open. Then I hit the bitch in her jaw, cracking her shit, and thus sending her to the floor. Reggie acted like he wanted to put hands on me, but I punched his ass in the face before he could even try, same shit I would have done to Maine's ass the other night after he had smacked me had my kids not walked into the room.

The lights came on in the club, and the music went off as a crowd quickly formed around me. I stomped the shit out of Joi, allowing my Retro Jordan covered foot to land wherever the fuck it pleased.

The entire time I was screaming at the top of my lungs, "Bitch, you wanna fuck my man? You fake ass bitch! You want that bum ass nigga, then take him! Good luck, bit—"

Security interrupted my rant. I fought with whichever one had grabbed me until I heard his familiar voice in my ear, "C'mon, Capri, chill out. Get the fuck out of here before the cops come. You got kids to go home to."

It was Kevin, the bouncer from the front door. I chilled out because he had never done shit to me, so I didn't want to fight him. Plus, he was right. I stopped fighting and allowed him to escort me out of the club.

As soon as the air hit me, he started trying to talk some sense into me, but I wasn't hearing it.

"I gotta go," I told him, turning to leave without allowing him to finish whatever common sense shit he was preaching to me. I didn't want to hear logic right now; I wanted to hear bones breaking. I had done that; Joi was first, and now Maine was next.

****

*Phwap!*

I had smacked the shit of Maine as I yelled, "Get the fuck up!"

He bolted out of his sleep. The first thing he did was reach for his gun, but I had had sense enough to grab it from his waist before I hit him. When he realized that it was missing, and then realized that I was pointing it at his head, his eyes bulged.

"Get yo' ass outta my room!"

"Yo, what the fuck?!" he shouted as he jumped to his feet. *Bet his ass ain't drunk no more.*

"You gawd damn right what the fuck?! What the fuck you been doin' talkin' to Joi?!"

Subconscious guilt gave him away. His eyes shamefully looked away from me, but he quickly tried to lie. "Man, you crazy as hell!"

"I'm crazy?! I'm crazy?!" As I dug in my pocket, I was sure I did look crazy as fuck. When I pulled my phone out of my pocket and unlocked it, he started to look at me curiously. He tried to come towards me, but I tightened my grip on the gun, and he hesitated.

"You ain't gon' shoot me," he told me.

"I ain't gon' shoot you?" I asked cynically. "*What's up with you, tho? You want to meet up with me? I wanna fuck you.*" I read their text messages as my eyes burned with tears. I wasn't sad; I was hurt. My circle had been so tight that it was a fucking line of three bitches only, but one was dead, the other was out of town, and the last had turned on me. I felt alone, and the nigga that was supposed to have my back didn't...*yet again*.

When he didn't even bother to deny it, it pissed me off more. "Get the fuck out!"

"I didn't even fuck her, though! I was dissin' her ass."

"But you initiated the shit!"

"Bab—"

"Don't fucking 'baby' me!" I squeezed the trigger, almost pulling it, but I realized that I couldn't go to jail for murder for so many reasons; the most important one being my kids. The second most important one was not going to jail over a bum ass nigga like him.

I walked towards the door, the gun still aimed at him as I swung it open. "Get the fuck out and don't never call me again." When he didn't move, I threatened, "Either walk out or have the police escort you out."

When he didn't believe me, I dialed out on my cell phone with it on speaker. "9-1-1, what's you—"

"Okay! Okay!" Maine insisted as he walked towards me and through the door. "I'm out, but this ain't over."

"Sorry, wrong number," I spoke into the phone before hanging up and slamming the door.

**** 

Hours later, though I had finally showered, I wasn't able to sleep. I lay in bed with my mind racing. The audacity of Maine's weak ass to even pull this shit was unbelievable to me. True enough, they hadn't actually fucked. But the deception was already there so they might as well had and probably would now. Even that thought fucked me up, so I tossed and turned for hours while my phone rang and rang. Some of the calls were from Joi. I had half the mind to answer so that we could meet up again and finish this shit, but I had kids to think of. Other unsaved numbers were calling me, and from the voicemails, I knew that it was Maine. He obviously had another cell phone that I didn't know about, and that only dug his grave even deeper. He was begging to talk to me and apologizing, but there was no talking or apologizing his way out of this shit. I had already had one foot out of the door. Now, I was completely gone for real.

At around 5AM my phone was still ringing. I went to turn it completely off but halted when I saw that it was Capone and immediately answered.

"Hello?"

"You're woke," he said sounding surprised. "You sound wide awake. You okay?"

I tried to sound as calm and cool as I could as I replied, "I'm okay. I just can't sleep." Then I quickly changed the subject before he could press the issue, "What's up with you? How was the Factory?"

"It was cool. Niggas just leavin'. I'm starving, though. I was hoping I could convince you to wake up and come with me, but you wide awake. You game?"

I grimaced silently.

*Lord, I ain't neva gon' get no sleep.*

For real, because how could I tell his sexy ass "no"? No matter my irritation or anguish with my situation, the sound of his rough, breathy, appealing voice was enough to give me the energy that the day had sucked out of me to do whatever his heart desired.

"Yea, I'm game."

"I'll be there in twenty."

I told him, "Okay," and hung up, reluctantly pulling myself out of bed and wondering what the fuck I was doing. Capone and I seemed to be going from zero to one hundred real quick. I did not want to jump out of one relationship and into another. When Maine and I met three years ago, it was as if we met, fucked, and never let go for three years. By the time I got to know him, I didn't like him. Despite the chemistry between us, I did not want that to happen to me and Capone.

I could not rebound. I could not make him fix what Maine had broken. Yet, he would be a great way to take my mind off of the bullshit.

# CAPONE

"So, let me get this right..." I rolled my eyes as Eboni continued to talk shit from the back seat. "We been at the club with hella bitches throwing mad pussy at you all night, Rachel been blowin' your phone the fuck up, but we are going to get *Capri* to take her to breakfast?"

I nodded confidently. "Yep."

"Whose is this nigga, and what happened to Capone?" I heard her ask Geno, who was in the backseat of my ride with her.

"Aye, Eboni," I called.

"Yes?"

"Fuck you, a'ight?"

Then the entire truck laughed, but I didn't find shit funny.

Me, Omari, Geno, Eboni and Jasmine were riding in my 2016, silver Infiniti truck. We had been at the Factory all night kicking it. Sleep was stalking all of us, but we had to soak up this liquor with a big breakfast so we wouldn't wake up with hangovers. I had asked Capri to come with us to the Factory, but she hadn't gotten off until eleven that night and said she was tired as hell from hanging with me all night the night before. I didn't press the issue because I didn't want to scare her away, but after walking out of the club into the sunlight and seeing my family all boo'd up, a nigga wanted something thick to sleep under. Rachel had been blowing me up, so had a few of my other dips, but my mind wasn't on any of them.

I was sure they didn't understand what the fuck had gotten into me. Shit, I didn't understand it myself, nor did I understand how I was so easily accepting it. I had been juggling pussy all of my life with no interest in finding "the one." But I guess a real man didn't hesitate when he found the right woman, even if he wasn't even looking for her.

However, I couldn't tell these shit talking ass motherfuckers in my truck any of that, so I simply sucked my teeth and said, "Ain't shit funny. Shorty just cool. I'm tryin' to get to know her."

That just made shit worse. They all fell the fuck out laughing! Straight cracking up like we were at the All-Star Comedy Jam or some shit.

"Get to know her?" Eboni mocked through laughs.

"Whaaat?" Geno taunted as he choked on his laughter.

Omari was damn near choking as well. "Awwww shit!"

Jasmine slapped my shoulder as she giggled. "Listen at this, nigga."

I just shook my head as we pulled into the parking lot of the motel.

"She stay in a motel?" Jasmine asked.

"Yea," Eboni answered for me. "She just left her nigga."

"She told you about that shit?" I asked.

"Yea, while at work last night."

"What did she say? Did he do anything to her?"

My voice changed from calm to beast mode real quick. I knew that Capri was hiding some facts behind why she had ended up in this motel. I really wanted to know if that punk ass nigga had done anything to her, but I knew that she saw in my eyes that it was best for her to keep that shit to herself.

"Listen to this nigga. Now you Robin Hood. Now you Captain Save A..." Jasmine stopped, knowing better than to refer to Capri as a hoe, even jokingly. Even though I tried to hide it, my demeanor subconsciously showed that I did not play when it came to Capri.

"So you fallin' for a chick with relationship issues? Damn..." I heard Geno say, but I was too busy sending Capri a text message, telling her that I was outside, to respond to Geno's ignorant ass.

But Eboni told him, "Shut up, Geno. She cool as hell."

"She must be, since this playa ass nigga falling for her," Jasmine giggled.

I fought the urge to smile as I watched out of the driver's side window. "Who said that I was falling for her, though?"

"Look where we are!" Omari laughed. "You havin' dates at five in the morning without gettin' no pussy and shit! You *def* fallin' for her, my nigga."

I had a bunch of shit to come back at this nigga with, especially pertaining to how Jasmine had come in and pussy whooped his ass, but the sight before me was leaving a nigga speechless. As I watched Capri walk towards the truck, something that Omari had told me came to mind. I had asked him after all he had been through, why and how did he even fall so hard for Jasmine. His answer was what I was feeling as I watched Capri smile at me while she seemingly glided towards me in a simple pair of leggings, a tank top, and Jordan's. It was exactly what Omari had described. Whatever she needed, I wanted to do it. I wanted to get my shit together just for her. I had never seen someone so beautiful in my life. She made me want so many things that I had never wanted before, like vacations with her and chill nights. I prayed that I would do nothing to mess up whatever this was between us. And I didn't know how the fuck I had gotten here, how I had a million bitches willing to fuck me right at that moment, but I was there with her... but I liked it.

# MAINE

After Capri had kicked me out of her room, I sat in the parking lot fuming and drinking, especially after I saw the remnants of my iPhone shattered into a million pieces on the concrete parking lot. Then I'd nodded off. I woke up attempting to sober up, and that was when I saw her coming out of the room at five in the morning like a hoe.

*This slut.*

This bitch was at my head about flirting with her girl, about telling her girl that I was straight on the pussy, but she had been doing dicks all along! Joi had been right all along. Even when Joi was telling me all that shit about Capri, I thought she was just lying to get some dick. Yea, I knew that Capri felt some type of way about me manning up and taking care of home in a way that wouldn't get me killed, but I never had any reason to think that it was another nigga until Joi started putting that shit in my head after that trip to Miami.

Since she'd come home from that trip, Capri had been giving me bullshit excuses about not giving me the pussy for months now, so I knew Joi was right.

Yea, I was bogus for initially coming at Joi, but honestly, Capri had been making me feel like less of a man and I, on some drunk shit, was out to prove her wrong. I entertained Joi's text messages and phone calls but respected my girl too much to do her that dirty.

But as I watched her walk up to an Infiniti truck and saw a nigga hurriedly hop out of the driver's side, walk up on her, grab her ass and kiss her like I used to, I figured I hadn't been doing her dirty enough. Capri thought this was a motherfuckin' game. There was no way I was going to let some nigga reap the benefits of having what I had groomed for three years.

"Hello?" I answered irritably as I put my foot on the gas and followed the Infinity truck. Luckily for me, I had a trap phone, despite Capri shattering my shit.

"Your girl found out about us."

"About us?" I sneered and actually took my eyes off of the truck. I looked at the phone like I was hearing things. "Ain't no 'us' to find out about, bitch!" Then I just hung up on Joi's dumb ass. That rich, stuck up bitch was so stuck on herself that she felt like a nigga should want the pussy, but I had shown her different, and she hated it.

As I followed two cars behind the Infiniti truck, I reached into my cup holder, grabbed my cup and took a big gulp of the Remy that I had been babysitting all day and night.

"She been playin' me all along," I muttered to myself.

It was cool, though; I was about to show Capri just how much she had me fucked up.

# CHAPTER 10

## CAPRI

Breakfast was a blur. At that point, I had been up for twenty-four long, excruciatingly dramatic hours. I fought to keep my eyes open as Eboni, Capri, Omari, Geno and Capone laughed and talked about their night at The Factory. I kind of wished that I had gone with Capone when he asked me to because had I gone, I wouldn't have known the true deception of Maine and Joi. Sometimes, what was understood didn't need to be discussed. I had already walked away from Maine, and it was obvious that Joi was not the down ass bitch that I needed in my corner. I didn't need to know the additional bullshit. It was just extra hurt to go along with the pain that I was already carrying around with me.

Luckily, during breakfast, Eboni invited me out to drinks with she and Jasmine later that week. I was happy to oblige since the only bitch left in this city that I fucked with was on my hit list. I needed a night out with the girls after all that had gone down, and if it had to be with some new girls, so be it.

By the time we staggered out of the IHOP and dropped Geno and Omari off at their car with the girls, I was begging for my bed. I was too exhausted to even appreciate the sexy way Capone looked when his eyes rode low from lack of sleep and exhaustion. As we arrived at the motel, I imagined not fucking him, but laying under him with his arm around me, as he'd done the night before, and getting some much-needed rest. It was now Sunday, and I knew that Aunt Dawn was taking the kids to church. I, at least, had until way after three o'clock to go get them and spend some time with them. I planned to sleep until then.

The lot of the motel was full, so Capone had to park a few feet away from my room. After he parked, he had the nerve to sit back and hesitate.

I stopped taking off my seatbelt and looked at him with confusion. "You aren't coming in?"

"You want me to?"

I sucked my teeth, cocked my head to the right dramatically, and looked at him like he was crazy. "Come on now. Stop playing with me."

Though his chuckles were deep, slow and groggy, they still were so adorable. A man as rough as him with tattoos all over his body that peeked out of the collar of his shirt, it was so cute to see him blush and giggle. I imagined that he didn't do it often, and I appreciated the moments that he let his guard down to do it with me.

"You just wanted to hear me say it, didn't you?"

He licked his lips, and his eyes drove into mine. "I just wanted to hear that you wanna still be around me."

My tired eyes continued to maintain the tension between our exhausted orbs as I said, "You know I don't want you to leave me."

That only made the erotic pressure between us worse. As I got out of the car, I silently prayed to the sexual gods, *Please don't let him try to fuck me. I'm too tired, and whenever I fuck him, I gotta give him the business. I'm too tired to give him the business. Please let him just go to sleep.*

I was crying silently on the inside as we made our way into the room. The way he looked at me up and down with his hands on the smallest part of my back and my ass, and the way he sat on the bed and stared at me as I removed my clothes, I knew that he was about to try to fuck me. I also knew that I was so weak for him and had waited for this moment to happen again for so long that I was going to, once again, put the need for sleep aside and give this man exactly what he wanted, exactly what my body needed, and exactly what my body had been craving since the last time he had taken it.

As I was slowly undressing, anticipating how my tired body could handle the dick that I saw pushing its way out of his jeans, he took off his shirt, and it was like a bitch *instantly* wasn't tired anymore. Suddenly, it was as if I had had the strongest cup of coffee with a shot of expresso because I was awake and ready to show that dick how much I had missed him.

*Gawd damn.* When we'd had sex in Miami, of course, we had been fully clothed. And when we spent the night together Thursday and Friday night, we had fallen asleep talking so were fully dressed when we woke up. Therefore, we had never seen one another's bare bodies.

We both fought not to stare at one another as each article of clothing left our body and hit the floor. I was amazed at the fact that though his body did not have as much mass as a guy like Omari, Capone was very much wide, cut up and defined. My mouth watered at the V shape that led to a few fine pubic hairs that stuck out over his boxers as he removed his jeans.

*I'm fucking him.*

That was it! I had made up my mind. I was trying to allow the man to treat me like a lady but fuck it! We had already had sex and at this point, there was no way that he was going to lay beside *me*, a woman that had not been manhandled since the last time he touched me, and expect me not to want to put his dick in my mouth! I was going to fuck that man that night. No exceptions. I was going to suck his dick like a fucking porn star and do things to him that would probably make him judge me in the morning, but I didn't give a fuck! I wanted it!

His phone rang, interrupting our eye fucking session. As he answered, "What up, bro?" I scurried into the bathroom to take a quick hoe bath, refreshing my intimate spots quickly in the sink, and prayed my body with peach fragrance mist. Then I looked myself over in the mirror. My Brazilian bundles no longer had much curl because of all that I had gone through that day, but I left my hair down because I now had a sexy bedhead look since some of my loose curls were falling in my face due to my off center part. I thanked the Lord that I had showered after Maine left and had grabbed a matching bra and panty set. I felt comfortable now as I grabbed the bathroom door knob and switched out, ready to get the dick that I had been fantasizing about.

But imagine my surprise when I looked up at Capone, and he was fully fucking dressed!

I didn't bother to hide my irritation. I stopped and folded my arms across my chest. He looked me up and down, paused at my breasts and then paused again at my hips. He came close to me, licking his lips, and wrapped his hands around my waist, allowing his hands to slowly run over my ass.

"Where are you going?" I whined.

"I'm just going right outside. Jasmine left her purse in my truck." I inwardly sighed with relief as he continued, "They are right around the corner. Be right back."

I smiled behind his back as he went towards the door, out of it, and closed it behind him. Then I rushed towards my phone and started to go through my music so that I could set the mood for what was about to go down. Even though I had made up my mind that I was going to fuck him, I could see in his eyes that he was definitely about to give me the fucking business! The gentleman that had been courting me was gone, and a beast had taken his place; the same beast that I met in Miami.

I was excited that we were finally about to relive Miami, but now we were going to be in a nice, comfortable bed instead of some dark, weird closet. No gunshots would interrupt us this time.

As I pressed play on the Trey Songz album, I started to swing my hips, my pussy gushing at the idea of what Capone was about to do to me.

♫ *She said she like it when I'm nasty*
*So I'mma give her what she ask for*
*Beat the pussy in the backseat*
*And she gon' suck it 'til her jaw sore*
*Yeah, yeah, yeah, yeah*

*Drinking your juice like the liquor*
*I eat that pussy for breakfast*
*Chop that peach up like a blender*
*She feel me deep in her chest*
*Top of the morn, she give me top*
*I be so deep in her neck*
*I be so deep, she be wet*
*We take the sheets out the bed* ♫

"Yaaas," I purred out loud as I let Trey Songz play. His "To Whom It May Concern" album was going to be the perfect soundtrack to our sex because my walls definitely remembered what Capone had done to me in Miami. My walls had not forgotten. They couldn't, and they were already leaking in anticipation of what he was going to do to them next.

I was in such a lust-filled, dreamy state that when I heard the knock on the door, I rushed towards it happily, not thinking twice when I swung the door open with a smile. But my smile quickly left when a dark, shadowy figure rushed towards me, put its hands around my neck, and squeezed so tightly that I couldn't scream.

"Bitch, you think you can pull a fucking gun out on me and get away with that shit while you in here fucking this nigga?"

I couldn't breathe; I could only reach up and claw at his fingers while he choked me so tightly that I could feel his fingers on the ridges of my esophagus. "First, I'm going to kill you, then I'm going to kill him," he foamed, spit flying from his clenched jaw as the nauseating smell of Remy filled my nose and made me sick to the stomach.

As we fell onto the bed, he let go of my throat, and I started to gasp for air. However, instead of choking me, he was now pummeling me with his fists over and over again, yelling obscenities and things that had obviously been on his mind as he sat outside waiting for this moment of punishment.

"Fuck you bitch! Trying to make me feel like I'm less of a man, like I ain't been taking care of you and those fucking kids! You want me to be a good father to them, and you don't even know who the fuck their father is!"

He was saying everything he knew that would piss me the fuck off. But no matter how much I tried to fight and dig my nails into his eyes, nothing I did overpowered him.

Then a loud thud thundered through the air, followed by a gunshot that pierced the air. I waited for the pain to take over my body. I was convinced that Maine had shot me until I felt him wince and roll over onto the bed next to me. I looked up with wide eyes and saw Capone aiming his gun at Maine. I frantically looked over at Maine and saw him clutching his leg. His crazy ass deserved every bullet that Capone looked like he wanted to put in him, but he was still the only father that my kids knew, and I didn't want to take that away from them after life had already given them so many disadvantages that they didn't deserve.

As I rushed towards Capone, I saw him ready to pull the trigger again. I stood in front of his gun, looking deep into his eyes. As I looked at him, I saw a man that I had never seen before but always knew was somewhere deep inside of him. The look of a killer was in his eyes. There was no guilt or remorse about what he intended to do either.

"Move, Capri."

"Please!" I begged him breathlessly. "Please don't kill him!"

"Urrrgh," Maine cried from the pain.

Capone looked at me like I was a fucking idiot for wanting to spare Maine's life. "Move, Capri. Don't make me move you for you."

My eyes bulged in surprise. Even in a fit of rage, he softened his approach towards me and said, "I would never hurt you. But I'm about to kill this nigga for hurting you. So move... *now.*"

Maine was still wincing in pain. I quickly looked up between him and Capone to make sure that Maine wasn't reaching for his own gun, but he must have stupidly left it behind because it was not in its usual spot on his waist. Blood was oozing from his knee as tears actually slid down the side of his face.

"Capone, please," I begged. "He's the only father that my children know. That's the only reason why I care. Please don't take that from them."

The murky look in his eyes, dark as an eclipse, went away at the mention of my kids. His eyes turned back to the soft, lovable expression that he usually gave me. "Get your things. We gotta get outta here." Then he turned to look at

Maine. His gun was still pointed at Maine's temple, so I froze as he threatened him. "If hear that you said anything to the police about this shit - If hear that you're treating her or those kids any different because of this - I am going to finish what the fuck I started. Don't try me. The only reason why you aren't going out of here in a body bag is because I want that pussy."

Had the situation not been so fucked up, I would have giggled a little. It was funny to see the straight up shitty look on Maine's face that forced passed his pain. I definitely knew then that I was right when I had made my choice to leave Maine. He was a bitch. He lay there not even fighting for me or fighting for his damn self.

Capone kept the gun on him as I quickly collected all of my things. I threw on a pair of jogging pants, a hoodie and gym shoes. Once Capone saw that I was dressed, he escorted me out of the room. There was no need to close the door behind us. Capone had kicked his way inside, causing it to hang off of the hinges as we stepped through the doorway.

On our way to his car, I couldn't tell you how many times I apologized, but he was so pissed that he wasn't saying a word. I felt so bad for putting him in the middle of me and my bullshit. Even though I'd had no idea that Maine would show up and do anything like that, I hated that Capone was even involved.

As we got into his car, I was totally convinced that this would probably be the last night that I saw Capone. The look in his eyes as he sat in the driver's seat and started the engine told me that he didn't have time for this shit. I didn't blame him at all.

"My car is over there," I told him softly as I pointed near the entrance of the lot. "There is another motel off of 159th Street. I can just go there. I can drive myself." I was mumbling like a scared little girl. I was avoiding his eyes, staring out of the window, afraid to look at the way he was probably condemning me.

I was completely taken aback when he said, "You don't have to stay at motels anymore. I got you."

My heart went out to his kindness and made me feel even worse. "Capone, I've caused you enough problems tonight. You don't have to do that."

"You didn't cause me any problems. I was meant to be here. If I wasn't here, there's no telling what would have happened to you. As a matter of fact, I apologize for letting my guard down and not noticing him coming to the room. I should have been on my shit."

I looked at him, not believing that he was actually sincere when he said that. He looked like a guard dog that had slept on his job and was punishing himself.

"I don't want you in any more motels. That shit ain't safe. We can come get your car in the morning. I got a place that you can stay—"

"Capone, you don't have to—"

He leaned towards me, stopping my words by simply placing his hand on my thigh. "Just let me take care of you, baby. That's what a man is supposed to do. Just let me take care of you."

I sighed and smiled secretly. He was right; this was what a man was supposed to do. And even though I wasn't used to it, I sat back in the seat and let him take care of me.

## CAPONE

Lucky for Capri, that lame ass nigga had his life.

On our way to the empty condo that I had near Lakeshore Drive, I asked her how often he had hit her. She promised that this had only been the second time; the first time being when she'd left and ended up at the motel. Luckily, there were no visible bruises on her, but we both knew that she would be sore in the morning from the quick beating.

Once we got to the condo, she was surprised that it was fully furnished and newly renovated. I had barely stayed in it, mostly staying at my spot in the city because I couldn't help but be in the hood. This lavish shit wasn't for me. As she looked around the twenty-three hundred square foot condo with wide eyes, I told her that it was one of my old spots that I had kept and planned on renting out, but never got to it.

"So how much is the rent?" she asked as she leaned on the back of the dark gray sectional.

"I can't charge you rent, ma."

"Yes, you can, and you will," she insisted with a smile as she softly folded her arms. "I appreciate you taking care of me and helping me get a place, but I just got my independence back, and I don't plan to give it up quite yet. Take care of me with something like dinner or quality time, but I'm finally able to pay my own rent, so I really want to."

That shocked the shit out of me and made me want her more, but tonight's event had snatched me out of that lust-filled cloud and brought me back down to reality. As I looked at this girl, who had impressed me with a few simple words, I realized that I didn't want to just fuck her. I didn't want just a night with her that would steer us away from getting to know one another and cause us to focus more on the sex. I didn't want her to end up like Rachel, Alicia, Adriana or any of the other chicks that I forgot about getting to know once they gave me the pussy.

I smiled at her with pride and told her, "You just keep saying and doing things to make me like you more."

She blushed. "Even after you had to damn near kill my ex-boyfriend tonight?"

As I walked toward her, I was still smiling. When she was close enough, I kissed her on her forehead and said, "Yeah, even though I had to damn near kill your ex-boyfriend tonight." Then I started to walk toward the front door, and I could see her obvious disappointment. "Make yourself comfortable. Take a hot bath and get some rest. I'll be back to check on you later."

With a voice full of uncertainty as she asked, "Promise?"

I nodded as I opened the door and said, "Promise," then I blew her a kiss before leaving.

# CHAPTER 11
*-a month later -*

## CAPRI

It was now May, a month later, and life seemed to be so different. It was as if in the blink of an eye, Capone had come into my life to take great care of me. The new condo was exactly what me and the kids needed. It was actually more than what we could have ever imagined. It was over two-thousand square feet and had four bedrooms, so the kids even had their own playroom. Even though I insisted on paying rent, Capone was charging me much lower than what the condo was worth. A place like that could have easily gone for nineteen hundred dollars a month in this city, but he was only allowing me to give him seven-hundred dollars, which he easily ended up giving right back to me through dinners, little gifts and date nights.

There was only one problem.

"He won't fuck me!"

Eboni's eyes bucked, and Jasmine almost choked on her Rum Punch. We were having lunch at Ja' Grill in Hyde Park. I had been hanging with these girls a lot over the past couple of weeks. Eboni and I had become pretty cool since I was now dating Capone and we worked together. More often, where there was Eboni, there was Jasmine, so I had become cool with her as well. Sometimes Jasmine's best friend, Tasha, tagged along too.

Because of our budding friendship, I had no problem telling Jasmine and Eboni, "Yes," every time they invited me out. Plus, it looked like Amiyah was never coming home. Every time she called me, she told me about another excuse that Shug had given her about life being better in St Louis. Amiyah was convinced that he was running from something but was too scared to press him to find out what it was. Even when I asked Maine, who had been surprisingly very cooperative with spending time with the kids and leaving me alone, he would just shrug his shoulders and act like he didn't know what was going on with Shug.

"Are you serious?" Eboni asked. "You guys haven't fucked yet?... I mean, besides in Miami." Then she giggled, tormenting me further.

I just looked at her and gave her a little smirk as she and Jasmine giggled uncontrollably across the table while they sipped their drinks. Once Eboni and I became cool outside of work, I was comfortable enough to tell her how I had met Capone. I was sure he had told Omari, so it would have eventually gotten to her anyway. She thought that it was fucking hilarious that two people who had met randomly at a club in Miami were now inseparable. I must say it was ironic, but the shit wasn't that damn funny.

However, yes, I was very serious; Capone hadn't fucked me yet. After that night he shot Maine, it was as if his focus was back on getting to know me. We spent a lot of time together and even spent the night together sometimes. But the most we had done was kiss. It was so bad that I was starting to think that the man wasn't attracted to me like that anymore and thought of me more as just a friend.

Just then, the waitress came to the table. "Are you guys okay? Anything else?"

Eboni answered, "You can get her..." She pointed at me, "... another rum punch. One-hundred proof, please."

"Unt uh!" I immediately disagreed shaking my head. "I already feel the first two. I don't need another one."

"Yea, you do," Eboni insisted. "Because you're about to go home and take that dick."

The waitress' eyes bucked, and I shrank with embarrassment.

The waitress continued to stand there, unsure of who to listen to.

"She wants another one," Eboni insisted. When the girl looked at me for approval, Eboni got gutter. "I said get her another damn drink, shit!"

I hurriedly added, "I'll take it. Thank you."

We all started to laugh as the waitress scurried away. Hanging with these girls had already taught me that Eboni did not play no motherfuckin' games, and Jasmine was right behind her, ready to fight her battles because they were so close. They called each other "baby mama," and they definitely acted like they were that to one another. They were definitely more than friends; they were family.

"Yes, Capri, you have to hurry up and fuck Capone so that you guys can be official in time for you to come to my wedding with him. My wedding is in *Jamaica*. You have to be Capone's date."

"Your wedding is in December, Jasmine. They will definitely be official by then. Do you see how this nigga looks at her?" Eboni asked.

"If that's the case, then why won't he fuck me?" I whined. "He obviously doesn't like me like that."

Eboni dramatically rolled her eyes into the back of her head as she told me, "Him not fucking you is letting you know how much he likes you. Do you know that if he didn't like you, he would have ran through your pussy, then just forgot about you and only remembered you on the nights that he wanted to run through that pussy again? I know Capone, and so does Jasmine. He is acting totally different with you, and it's because he actually gives a fuck about you. But if you want just as much fucking as there is caring, you just are going to have to take the dick and pray that it doesn't change things in the morning."

"But he won't change, I promise you," Jasmine added. "He is a street nigga to his soul, but for the past month, you have had his ghetto ass at the finest restaurants, at Navy Pier, and the lake front. The man is trying to woo you. He deserves the pussy. *Give it to him.* Take the dick."

I sat there still unsure no matter what they'd said. Capone and I had been so perfect. We had actually established a friendship that I didn't want to ruin with sex, which always seemed to complicate things. Capone and I were the easiest and sweetest thing that had happened to my life in a long time. I didn't want to fuck that up just because I wanted to bust a nut. I knew that I wouldn't change afterward, but I was scared that Capone would. I had been holding out just as long as he had because I was scared. I was scared that the Netflix and chill nights, the dates downtown, and the random bouquets of flowers would turn into… *Maine.*

My eyes fell on Eboni, silently questioning her if I should do this. She and Jasmine were older than me and had more experience with these men. They knew Capone like the back of their hands, so I trusted them as Eboni looked me dead in my eyes and insisted, *"Take the dick, bitch."*

# CAPONE

"I can't believe we can't find this motherfucka! Is he the Illuminati or some shit?" I barked as I sped through the city. "This shit is starting to get on my motherfuckin' nerves. I'm ready to go shoot up any goddamn body related to him at this point!"

I heard a deep, evil chuckle on the other side of the phone before Carlos told me, "You know I'm down for whatever. But DBD don't operate like that. You and Omari don't kill innocent people. So calm down and let me take care of this shit, my nigga. I got you. Even though it's taking some time, this shit is going to be bittersweet in the end. You will get your vengeance."

"Make that shit happen then, man. Find that nigga."

"I got you, boss."

Omari eyed me as I ended the call and dropped the phone into my lap. I was so irritated that I wanted to throw my phone across the hospital room.

I was with Omari visiting Fred, who was in an induced coma after another surgery. He had undergone surgery after surgery to repair the damage that the two bullets to the chest had caused. My nigga was suffering, and that made me feel like that was worse than death as I stared at him. The few times he opened his eyes and said anything to us, it was as if he wanted nothing more in the world than to get up from that bed and turn up with us again, smoke another blunt with us again, pop bottles with us again. He was strong and holding on, and I was convinced that he was going to walk out of this hospital eventually.

Yet, it was my mission that once he walked out of this hospital, all of his suffering would not have been in vain. I wanted to have his life even better than it was when he left, and I wanted to take the life of the person that had put him here.

"Why don't you go home and see your girl? Ain't you supposed to be meeting her at her crib?"

Omari was right; if I had sat in the hospital another hour, staring at Fred, who was not even breathing on his own, I was going to defy the codes of our organization and start shooting anybody I knew that was associated with the motherfuckers that did this. I wanted Fred to wake up so badly for selfish reasons. Yeah, I wanted my nigga to be okay, but I also wanted him to be able to describe to me the other person that was with Shug that night. But every time he was conscious, he was too weak and could barely speak, so the doctors insisted that we didn't force him to. Then something else in his body would go wrong, and he would go back in surgery. Now, he was in an induced coma so that he could heal without interruption.

I sighed, stood and told Omari, "You're right. Let me get the fuck out of here. You comin' too?"

"In a minute."

Omari had been spending a lot of time at Fred's bedside. It was as if he wanted to watch every breath that Fred took to make sure that he didn't die. This was another reason why I was so fucking angry. Fred didn't deserve this, but Omari didn't deserve to go through losing another person close to him either. Rico was *my* boy; he was like my brother. I had grown up with him. But Omari had grown close to Fred over the years that he had worked for us. He was family to us as well, and my nigga Omari couldn't afford to lose not one more family member.

"A'ight, man. I'm out then."

We shook up, and then I bounced, fighting the urge to wreak havoc on the city. I needed to be close to my girl. It was like Capri was the kryptonite to my murderous wrath. The moment I touched her black skin, it was as if I calmed down, darkness left my eyes, and I could think clearly.

And that was what happened the moment that I walked through the door of her condo. I only had a key because when I insisted on giving her the spare one that I had, she wanted me to keep it. I noticed how quiet the condo was so I assumed that Nikki and Nicholas were asleep by now, especially since it was after ten o'clock at night. I expected to find Capri in the bathtub, because that was how she usually ended her days once the kids went to sleep.

But when I entered the master bedroom, what I found was a completely naked black beauty lying on her stomach with one leg bent slightly, giving me a peek of that pretty pussy as she stared at me seductively. I had to lean against the door frame to get control of myself. This was the first time that I was able to see every inch of her bare skin. Over the last couple of weeks, I might have caught her at least in her bra and panties. But now I was able to see her tender nipples and the crack of her ass, which led to a small glimpse of her pussy lips. My dick was hardening in my Robbins shorts as she stared at me with a seductive smile. I had known this day was coming. No matter how much I had tried to force us to get to know one another beyond our sexual night in Miami, the sexual tension between us was so fucking unbearable. I really wanted to show her that this wasn't about pussy to me, but fuck it. Considering the day that I had had, if my baby wanted the dick, she was going to get it.

I tried to act cool, as if I wasn't super excited to be getting ready to get in this pussy. I walked into the room like the last couple of weeks without getting any pussy at all had been easy. Every woman in my phone had been blowing me up, wondering what the fuck was going on with me, and all of them had assumed right; I had moved on to the next. A woman seemed to know when a man had settled down, and when she had been fucking that man for years and he didn't settle down with her, that was worse than a smack in the face to her. I was hearing the offense felt by every woman that I had disowned with every voicemail and text message that was left on my phone from one random bitch or another, especially Alicia and Rachel. But what they didn't even know was that yes, I had moved on, but my dick was still dry because this woman lying in this bed, looking like nothing but heaven, was important to me for a reason that I didn't even know nor could I even explain.

"That's what you on?" I asked her coolly as I climbed into the bed.

She sat up on her knees. Her perky, DD breasts

bounced with every movement and my mouth watered, wanting them motherfuckers in my mouth so bad.

She had the nerve to take my amazement as hesitation and asked sadly, "You don't want to, do you?"

When she sighed dejectedly, I smelled the liquor on her breath despite the Colgate that she had attempted to mask it with. I smiled, knowing that this was all liquid courage, but appreciated it. When I smiled, she relaxed and started to take off my tee shirt. "Please say you want it. Because I miss it so much."

A nigga had to exhale on the low because every word she said was making my dick hard as fucking brace. My only hesitation with fucking her was my ability to be inside of her for more than a few seconds before I bust prematurely from weeks of anticipation and now current complete fucking awe.

As she pulled my shirt over my head, I asked her, "How much you miss it?"

Those pretty eyes, with slits that matched mine, stared directly into mine with so much intensity that I could have busted a nut right then.

She began to unbutton my shorts and bring them down to my knees with her eyes still on me. She was not going to answer my question verbally. She was going to answer it physically. I knew that as she grabbed my dick out of my boxer briefs and began to stroke it. I knew that I was gone off of this girl when the simple touch of her small soft hands on my long, hard dick damn near made me orgasm right then. I thanked God that I was able to keep my composure, but that gratitude was premature. I was about to buss instantly when she bent down and her big ass heavily dropped into a heart in front of me, which I wanted to put my face right in the middle of. As she swallowed my dick, I knew that her wet mouth was definitely going to be the end of me. The neck she was giving me was incredible. Her throat felt like home. I could only lay back on the bed and lose my fingers in her hair as I tried to convince myself, *Don't fall in love, nigga.*

# CHAPTER 12

## CAPONE

I got that first nut out of the way real fast unapologetically. I came in that magnificent throat, expecting her to jump away, but she didn't. She swallowed and even lapped up the droplets of my nut that she had missed, and that's when I knew she was my mine.

After that nut left my body, she continued to suck me until I got hard again, which didn't take long because a nigga was ready. I put her on her back, threw her legs on my shoulders and punished her for every day, every moment, every second, that this pussy hadn't been mine since the moment that I had claimed it in Miami.

"Shit! Baby, yes!" she breathed. "Give me that dick! If feels so fucking good in my pussy!"

Her moans and lustful cries sounded like angels

having sex. Every noise she made and every word she said was just encouraging my dick to get harder and harder as I swam inside of her.

"Come here," I demanded, but before she could do as I said, I grabbed her by her waist and flipped over. Now she was on all fours, her back arched to perfection. I shoved my dick into her tight hole, and she immediately started throwing her phat ass back on my dick. I leaned back, bracing myself against the bed and allowed myself to enjoy the view of the jiggle that bounced back against my pelvis.

"Fuuuuuck," I groaned. I was fighting the urge to buss again. Her pussy, *my pussy*, was so wet that it was unbelievable. Her juices were dripping all over my dick and down my balls. This was way more than the pussy that I had gotten in Miami, way more than I expected, but a nigga was still grateful. And I was showing her how grateful I was by giving her all of my inches blatantly, with no interruptions, no hesitations, and no reluctance. She was getting every piece of me, exactly what she wanted, and she wasted no time showing me her approval.

"Yeeeeesssss, Capoooooone," she purred just as loud alarm sounds could be heard through her open bedroom window.

I attempted to stroke through the loud chaos, but I

recognized the alarm to be my own, so it was hard for me to keep giving her these good, deep strokes while wondering why the alarm on my Range Rover truck was going off in the private parking lot in the back of the building.

She heard it as well. She felt my pace slow, so she told me, "Please, don't stop, Capone. Please, baby? This dick feels *so* fucking good."

I tried to keep fucking past the wailing sound of the alarm, figuring that maybe a large animal had triggered it, but then the sound of shattering glass pierced the air.

I jumped out of the pussy before I even knew it.

"Gawd damnit!" she cursed. I could see her kicking the air and punching the bed out of the corner of my eye as she fussed, "Why is it that every time we have sex or are about to have sex, something interrupts us? It's God! We're not supposed to be having sex!"

As I ran to the window, I told Capri, "Maybe it's the devil. Don't think so negative."

I looked out of the window and realized that I was right. It truly was the devil, dressed in a red maxi dress with a bat in her hand. I cringed, realizing that Rachel had most likely made me lose that good pussy that I had just jumped out of for good.

*I'm knockin' her ass out.*

I rushed away from the window and threw on my clothes as Capri's eyes asked me so many questions that I think she was too scared to ask me verbally.

Now fully clothed, I told her, "I'll be right back. I'll handle this. Don't move."

*I'mma kill this bitch!*

I was seriously considering putting my hands around Rachel's neck and squeezing until she couldn't breathe anymore. I didn't give a fuck about my truck, which was obviously getting dismantled as I ran down the steps and continued to hear crashing and thuds in the back of the building. I could have bought five more trucks the very next day. What I cared about was the fact that this bitch had had the nerve to even show up. She knew what our relationship was, despite what she wanted. Bitches like this made me sick, and they didn't even deserve to breathe the same air as women like Capri.

As soon as I barged through the back door and she saw my face, Rachel started to spazz out. "So this why you not fucking with me?!" *Bam!* She swung the bat and added two more dents to my sexy ass, blacked out, ninety-thousand-dollar Range Rover. "You fuckin' the bitch *good* too! I heard the bitch screamin' way out here!"

I gasped when I saw the condition of my truck. Every

window and light was shattered. The body was ruined. When she saw the anguish in my eyes, she laughed. She was probably getting a kick out of this since this was the most vulnerable she had ever seen me.

"Yea, motherfucker! I hurt your truck just like you fucking hurt my heart!"

I actually saw tears in her eyes as she screamed and stared at me. I couldn't believe that she actually had real life feelings for me, despite me telling her over and over again that we were nothing more than sex and friends. The problem with women like her is that they think they can fuck and suck a man into being in a relationship. To me, sometimes it looked like that shit really worked. I saw so many of my homies in relationships that they didn't even want to be in, that the woman created in their own mind, and my homies felt stuck, especially after a kid came into the picture. I feared that that would be my reality, and that's why I never allowed myself to settle down. But when I was with Capri, I *wanted* to be with her. Without even getting the pussy for the past couple of weeks, I actually thought about being with her for the long run. *That* was real shit; not the sex plus time equals feelings situationship that Rachel had put herself in.

"I ain't touched you in weeks so what the fuck you

thought this was?" I fumed as I charged towards her. "I never said I wanted to be with you! It ain't my fault that you thought pussy was going to change my mind! I fuck a lot of pussy. I didn't want to be with those pieces of pussy no more than I wanted to be with you!"

She was so stunned that she immediately dropped the bat and clutched her chest. I wasn't afraid of her using that bat on me anyway. She knew my life and knew how the fuck I rolled. But what I didn't know was why she was acting so fucking dramatic and shocked. These were not words that she was hearing for the first time. It was what I told her time and time again, every time she mentioned being in a relationship. I had even told her that I was fucking other people, but that only seemed to be an initiation of a competition to her. She thought she would come out on top. And I could see in her eyes the feeling of defeat, now that she realized that someone else had won.

"I was there for you!" she cried.

"So was my other friends!"

Suddenly, she was no longer looking at me. She was looking behind me with jealous eyes. I cringed, reluctant to turn around, knowing who and what Rachel was looking at. Before I could even acknowledge Capri, it was like Rachel had seen red; she sprinted passed me and toward Capri like a fucking maniac. She was so quick that when I went to grab her, she slipped out of my grasp before I could even snatch her ass up. Capri, who had thrown on a pair of jeans and a t-shirt and her hair up in a bun, had a look in her eyes that said she was ready for some action.

They attacked one another like raging cats. Rachel had pissed me off so much that when Capri went in and started to beat her ass the moment that they were within arm's length, I let them go at it for a few seconds. I couldn't put my hands on Rachel, but I was glad that Capri was giving her the business. Every punch that Capri landed was for every dent, every scratch and every shattered window that that crazy bitch had put in my truck. In the meantime, I snatched up the bat and threw it as far as I could into the field behind us.

Rachel attempted to overpower Capri but failed. They were about the same size. I loved a woman that was BBW, and Capri was definitely that, in addition to being a savage. It turned me on to see her plummeting the shit out of Rachel. Every punch she threw was for me. It was what I wanted to do, and I was happy to watch it unfold for only a few seconds before I finally broke them up.

"Stupid ass bitch! Stay the fuck away from my crib with your crazy shit!" Capri threatened as I pulled her off of Rachel.

I held her in my arms and literally carried her away, towards the back door.

Rachel struggled to stand. I left her there as I carried Capri into the building. She wasn't even fighting me as I opened the door and sat her inside of the building. I closed and secured the back door and stared at her, not knowing what to say as she attempted to catch her breath. Her pretty face didn't have a scratch on it, which I would have guessed since she never gave Rachel the upper hand.

I figured only a sincere apology could fix this. "I'm so sorry—"

She stopped me. "I don't want to hear it," she breathed. "I heard everything."

"So you know I'm not fucking her, right? I ain't touched that girl or nobody else, I swear. I know this shit looks bad, but please believe me, ma." She was just looking at me, still attempting to catch her breath, not saying anything, so I was disappointed and even more pissed off at Rachel. "If you want me to leave, I'll leave—"

"Leave? Who said I wanted you to go anywhere?" she asked, as her lustful grin reappeared. "Fuck that bitch. I want the rest of that dick. C'mon."

# MAINE

*Fuck!*

When I saw that the door of my aunt's home had been kicked in, I knew that something was wrong. I couldn't run because my knee was still healing, so I limped as fast as I could towards the house. I had just left at around eleven that night to drop off an eight-ball to a customer and had only been gone for an hour. But considering the small amount of time it took me to hit a spot, as I walked through the broken door, I knew that I had been gone long enough for something to have gone terribly wrong.

That was confirmed as I walked down the hall and saw my aunt's body lying in a pool of blood in the living room.

"Oh shit!" I gasped as I ran towards her. But there was nothing that I could do. By the look of the three holes in her upper body, I knew she was dead. I immediately thought about my stash spot. Frantically, I ran towards the back of the house and into the back room where I kept the bricks and cash that I had stolen from DBD in the back of a closet in an old TV.

"Fuck!" Nothing was left. Of what I had left of the work and cash that me and Shug had stolen, everything was gone.

I kicked the wall in anger, boiling. "FUCK! Fuck! Fuck!"

That was all that I'd had. I had risked so much only to have a couple of hundred dollars in my pocket. This situation had me so spent that I felt sick to the stomach as I dialed 9-1-1 and left the room.

"Hello? What your emergency?"

"My... my aunt is dead," I stuttered in disbelief. "It looks like—like she got robbed. I don't know."

"Did you check her pulse?" the operator asked.

"Yes, ma'am," I lied. I hadn't checked her pulse. There was no need.

"Is there someone in the house still?"

"No," I breathed as I stared helplessly at my aunt's body as I walked up the hall.

"Okay. Help is on the way, sir."

I hung up, knowing that nothing could help my aunt as I stepped over her body towards the front door.

Once outside, I sat on the porch with head in my hands. I knew that one of my own had done this. Only a few people knew about this spot and where my stash was.

I would have thought that this was DBD's doing, but they didn't roll like this; they especially didn't kill women. And though I had recognized Capone the day he'd shot me, I knew that he didn't know me from a can of paint. But Shug had pointed him out to me in a few pictures of his before we hit the spot.

That was why I had been playing so nice with Capri. I had even let her come to the crib we once shared to get all of her things without any argument from me. Shit, I even helped her move the shit. I figured that if I was still the good father she wanted for the kids, if Capone ever pillow-talked and told her about knowing who had killed his boy and robbed his spot, she would at least give me a heads up.

Yet, DBD didn't know anything as of yet. I knew that because they hadn't done this. DBD was very meticulous in how they handled things. If this had been DBD, I would have been dead on that floor, not my aunt. This shit was messy, sloppy and something only niggas I knew would do.

At that moment, I regretted that Shug was gone. He had been my right hand, figured out shit when I couldn't, and saw things that I didn't. I had obviously missed something with the little niggas that I'd had serving this dope for me. I was sleep and that had caused my aunt her life and me the little riches that I had managed to acquire.

# AMIYAH

"Did you have to kill her?!" I shrieked as I sped down the expressway. "Fuck!"

This wasn't what was supposed to happen. Shug and I were supposed to slip into town, rob Maine and get the fuck out of Chicago. Killing someone, especially his aunt, was not on the fucking program!

I was way too exhausted after making the five-hour drive this morning, and now this anxiety matched with my exhaustion was literally making me shake as I drove at seventy miles an hour. I wished that Shug's license wasn't suspended so that I could at least freak out without having to focus on the road. But I was to be damned if he got pulled over and searched under suspicion because he was a black thug driving a trap car on the expressway. Driving without a license was one thing, but the three bricks and roughly eight thousand in cash that we had stolen from Maine was a whole 'nother level of felony.

I took a deep breath, attempting to calm down.

"I had to do it," Shug said sadly. "She saw our faces."

"I thought you said she wasn't home!"

"Her car wasn't in the driveway!"

Fuck, man! This was what I deserved for being with some stupid, low budget corner nigga. I thought of Capri's budding relationship with Capone and felt envious. She had hit the jackpot with that nigga, let Shug tell it.

After being in Saint Louis for so long, I had threatened to leave if Shug didn't tell me what was going on. It was obvious that he was so stressed out and fucked up in the head that me leaving him would only make him feel worse, so as I stood at the door of his mother's house with my bags in hand, he broke down and finally told me what happened.

I had already known that he and Maine must have hit a lick when he started buying shoes, jewelry, taking me out and had even upgraded his car to a used Challenger. But I couldn't believe that Maine and Shug had gotten so thirsty that they had robbed DBD. Apparently, it was known amongst the hustlers in Chicago not to fuck with DBD because, first of all, they didn't fuck with anybody else. They made their money and stayed in their lane. They weren't like these dumb asses out here shooting up blocks and killing innocent people. Their focus was on money. Because of Capone's deadly reputation, one of the heads of the organization, street niggas definitely knew of them and knew not to fuck with them. But chicks like me and Jasmine knew nothing of DBD or Capone because we had barely made it up the food chain to fuck with men like Capone or anyone in DBD.

When Shug shared all of this with me, it boggled my mind as to why he would be stupid enough to follow Maine into that trap house and commit that robbery and murder. It had then made total sense to me why he suddenly wanted to move to Saint Louis, and it pissed me off that I wasn't on my own two feet sturdy enough to stay in Chicago anyway, because I definitely didn't want any parts of this shit. I had agreed not to share any of this with Capri, especially now that, ironically, she was fucking Capone. Capri was my bitch, but this was my life we were talking about as well. This was the type of shit that had gotten our girl, Teresa, killed in high school, so I had to think of myself first.

Since I loved this stupid ass nigga and wanted my life, I had to keep his secrets. And because I wasn't working and only had a high school diploma and no work history, I had to stay with my man. Plus, my goofy ass loved the dummy. He had taken care of me for years, so I felt obligated to take care of him. That was why when he was also honest with me about not making any money in Saint Louis, having had run through the money they stole, and wanting to rob Maine, I was game. Shit, Shug was right; Maine was stupid as fuck for killing Rico and shooting Fred, and it wasn't fair that Shug had had to start his life over because Maine wanted to be stupid.

He had been ornery when he left, refusing to take any of the dirty drugs that Maine had offered him to leave. But now, weeks later and broke, he was regretting it. He knew what Maine had left because Maine's goofy ass told him everything every time he talked to Shug.

I was all for accompanying him back to Chicago, and even followed him into the house to look out while he went through Maine's aunt's house for Maine's stash, but I was *not* on deck for fucking murder!

# CHAPTER 13
*-a month later -*

## CAPRI

Capone and I had been messing around for a little over two months now. After that girl, Rachel, had showed up at my house, I honestly took a step back emotionally. I was already intent on taking things slow with Capone. I had just gotten out of a three- year relationship and didn't want to jump right into another one. It seemed as if he wasn't used to being as involved with a woman as he was with me. That was proven when Rachel showed up at my house and I heard their conversation as I stood at the back door. After hearing everything they had said, I was scared of falling for Capone, even more than I had, just for him to then suddenly turn back into a man whore. So, we were still hanging out, having crazy, good sex, but I was more so focused on my kids and my job and was enjoying my time with him, which was frequent. I wanted my man loyal, nasty, praying, low-key, and all about me and his money. Capone seemed to have all of those attributes on lock, but after that conversation he and Rachel had, I questioned his ability to be loyal and to be all about me.

Oddly, I had been seeing Maine more and more. He was spending a lot more time with the kids and less time in the streets. His aunt had been killed in a robbery a month ago, and even though he didn't admit it, I knew that it had something to do with him. The guilt had been all over his face at her funeral. When I would ask him why someone would rob his aunt, he would avoid the question with a nonchalant answer, but it seemed as if he was righting his hidden wrongs by being a better person to the people around him. He was almost turning into the man that I used to love, and it was nice to see the change in him. Had Capone not been fucking my brains out, I probably would have been convinced to hang out with Maine one-on-one as he had been asking over and over again. But I knew better than that. Maine always changed temporarily, then never learned his lesson and went back to his old ways.

"Whew, girl! I'm so glad its lunch. I'm starving' like a hostage," Eboni joked as we walked towards the Emergency Room entrance.

"Where are we going?"

"Let's go to Checker's on 55th."

"I gotta eat light. Since my aunt has the kids this weekend, Capone is taking me to dinner," I explained.

The sound of that made me sigh with relief. While I was living in that motel, I had gotten a taste of freedom from the kids that I hadn't felt since they had come into this world. There was even more relief because I had assurance that they were safe since my mother had gone on yet another hiatus. She had been gone for two months at this point. She was answering the phone for my aunt but would never come home, so I was ready to have a kid-free, stress-free, and dick-filled weekend!

"Oooooo! Somebody's gon' get some *dick* tonight!" Eboni teased.

I laughed but burst her bubble. "Probably not tonight. He has some meeting to go to after dinner."

Eboni nodded. "Oh yea. Jasmine mentioned something to me about that."

"What's it about?"

"Girl, you know them niggas ain't tellin'."

When I met Capone, I was no fool. I knew that he sold drugs, and I knew better than to attempt to get all in his business by asking him questions. But as we spent more and more time together, it was confirmed that he wasn't some regular dealer that sold ounces out of some trap house. He was a distributor and had to be distributing *a lot* of product, seeing how he and Omari were nowhere near short on coins.

As my cell phone rang, I glanced at my phone, which was in my hand, saw that it was Capone and answered on my wireless headset. "Hey, baby."

"What up, though?"

"Hey, Capone!" Eboni cut in.

"Now what if it wasn't him?" I asked her.

"She know it ain't nobody else," he gloated.

She sucked her teeth, waved her hand dismissively and said, "Girl, ain't no other 'baby' callin' you..."

My attention was taken away from her and Capone when I recognized the car speeding into the emergency room circle driveway behind an ambulance. Paramedics were currently pulling a patient out of the back.

My heart began to beat fast as I saw my auntie jump out of the driver's side of her Buick. As she rushed to get Nicholas out of the backseat, I immediately assumed that something had happened to my mother and wondered where Nikki was.

As my aunt and I both ran towards the back of the ambulance, I snatched Nicholas out of her arms. "What happened?!" I shouted at my aunt.

Eboni looked on curiously and shaken. I myself started to shake as the paramedics pulled the gurney out of the ambulance.

Instead of my mother laying on the gurney, it was Nikki.

I gasped and immediately started to cry and scream as I rushed towards the gurney. "What happened?! What the fuck happened?!"

Auntie Dawn tried to settle me down by grabbing my shoulder. I snatched away as tears started to leak from my eyes.

"Ma'am, we need you to move back," I heard the paramedic sternly say.

I was starting to hyperventilate as I quickly looked over her body while they rushed by me. She was conscious and crying, and I saw no blood or bruises, however I still didn't relax.

As my aunt and I rushed into the emergency room behind the paramedics, I shot daggers at my aunt. "Say something!"

Her hesitation told me everything but she finally admitted, "I left them with your mother for an hour so that I could run to the sto—"

I spazzed. "You left them with my mother?! What was

she doing there?! Why would you do that?!"

"She just showed up earlier. She wanted to take a bath and eat, so I let her. I had to run to the store," she replied with anguish in her eyes. "I didn't want to take them with me. When I came back..." She then lowered her voice to a whisper, "...she had left them home alone and Nikki was lying at the bottom of the stairs crying."

I began to hyperventilate as we rushed through the double doors of the trauma unit. "Oh my God," I cried.

Tears were in Aunt Dawn's eyes as she told me, "I don't know what's wrong with her. She was just lying there crying, so I called 911. I- I don't...I'm so sorry, Capri."

I had to bite my tongue. I didn't want to disrespect her, but it was stupid as hell for her to leave my children with my crackhead ass mama. Aunt Dawn knew that my mother was irresponsible; that was why she had raised me for most of my life. I was clueless as to why she even still allowed my mother to live with her. My mother was constantly in and out, using my aunt for a warm bed when she got tired of sleeping on the streets, or for a few dollars when she ran out of the money she got panhandling and stealing. The fact that she would leave my kids with somebody like that was astonishing to me, but I kept that to myself in order to calm my nerves as we attempted to follow the paramedics into the trauma room.

"I'm sorry, but you can't come in," the nurse told us nicely. "Please wait in the waiting room. The doctor will be out as soon as he can."

That bitch could have got these hands, but I had to calm down and realize that she was right. I had worked in this setting for so long that I should have already known better, but my motherly instincts were taking over.

I solemnly followed my aunt and Eboni out of the waiting room. Then I realized that I had been on the phone with Capone before I saw my baby in that ambulance.

I looked at my cell phone and saw that the call had ended. I wanted to call him back, but I was too caught up and worried to even do so.

As we sat in the emergency waiting room, my aunt apologized over and over again. Since she looked so guilt stricken, I kept my mouth closed and just prayed for my baby. There was no telling what had happened in that house since she had been all alone with a three-year-old. All I could do was pray that there was nothing terribly wrong with Nikki.

For twenty long minutes, I stared at those double doors and waited for the doctor to come out. I was becoming antsy, crying and leaning on Eboni's shoulder as a shadowy figure appeared above me. I looked up, relieved and expecting to see the doctor, but all I saw was a worried

Capone.

Suddenly, a sigh of relief left my body so hard that everyone around me could hear it. I immediately stood and jumped into his arms. He wrapped them tightly around me and kissed my cheek.

"I heard everything. Is she okay?"

"I don't know," I cried into his chest.

I couldn't believe that he was there, but knowing him, I couldn't believe that I didn't think that he would have stopped everything to be there for me after hearing what happened.

As we embraced, I even heard him saying a prayer, asking God to make everything okay. My heart melted as this man, as rough as he was with canvases of tattoos all over his body, most likely a gun in his pocket, and a history of God-only-knows what type of violence and crime, held me tightly and continuously kissed my cheek as he prayed. Beyond my worries for my baby, I thanked God for this man. Even though I did not know his purpose in my life, he had already turned out to be such a blessing.

# CAPONE

When I heard the turmoil in Capri's voice, I rushed out of Omari's crib and raced over to the hospital. Hearing Capri's screams and sadness scared the fuck out of me. I had post-traumatic stress or some shit after Rico's murder and watching Fred fight for his life. I couldn't take anybody else close to me dying or suffering. So I sat in the emergency room with Capri, holding her and praying to God that she would not have to suffer the way that I had, the way that I had watched Omari suffer. Nobody should have to go through that, and I didn't want to see any hurt come to Capri.

As I held her, I realized how much she meant to me, even how much her kids had meant to me as I had gotten to know them over the past two months. Even though I wasn't the relationship type, I wondered if a committed relationship was developing between me and Capri. As I held her, I wondered if I was ready to protect her and her kids the way a man in her life should. I wondered if I could keep her away from the pain that Omari and Rico and Fred's families were dealing with. I was the man that was deep in the streets, and I didn't want to put that type of suffering on the woman that I chose to commit myself to.

Six hours later, everything was a little better as me, Eboni, Capri and the kids walked tiredly into Capri's condo. It had been a long day, but our prayers were answered. Capri was carrying Nikki, who had suffered a bruised rib, sprained ankle, and mild concussion from her fall. Though her injuries were minor, Capri blamed herself for putting her kids in the same situation that she had been in when she was their age.

During our pillow talk conversations, Capri had told me how, when she was younger, she would go days without eating and in the house alone when she was in her mother's care. Even when she stayed with her auntie, her mother would come around, causing confusion with the way that she stole from them and brought stress to the entire household with her addiction.

As Capri went to lay Nikki down, I took Nicholas out of Eboni's arms.

"That was scary as fuck," Eboni said with a sigh of relief.

I tiredly shook my head. "I know right?"

I wasn't the only one with post-traumatic stress. Eboni's friend, Aeysha, had been murdered in 2013. Ayesha had also been Omari's pregnant girlfriend, so Eboni had to watch him suffer as she suffered herself. Since Eboni had been fucking around with Omari behind Aeysha's back and had also been pregnant at the time, she had felt hella guilt on top of her loss. The baby that Aeysha had been carrying survived the shooting, but she was also killed a few months later. And when Omari found out that his side bitch, Simone, had killed both Aeysha and their daughter, Eboni had been right there, consoling him and making sure that he didn't off himself as she attempted to keep herself together too. I had been there as well, but I couldn't break down; I'd had to hold down the organization that Omari and I had built.

So Eboni and I had been through enough loss and tragedy to last a lifetime, and today had taken us back to some fucked up memories. The hurt and anguish of those memories was all over our faces as our silence and eyes spoke volumes.

"I know you need to get home to your kids. Thanks for being there for her."

Eboni smiled sadly. "It's okay. Jasmine picked them up for me. But I do need to go get them." Then she sighed. "Tell Capri to call me in the morning to let me know how she and

Nikki are doing."

I nodded in agreement as she left. Holding Nicholas in one arm, I locked up and went towards the kid's room. When I didn't see Capri inside, I made an about-face and headed towards her bedroom. Inside, she was spooning with a sleeping Nikki on the bed.

As I lay Nicholas in bed with them, she told me, "Thank you," so groggily that I knew she would be sleep soon. "I know you're tired. I'm sorr—"

"You better not," I threatened her softly. "You don't have to apologize."

She kept quiet and just stared at me. Since Rachel showed up at her house a month ago, Capri had been way more cautious with what was going on between the two of us. We still kicked it and fucked like rabbits, but there was now a wall around her heart.

I was ready to break that motherfucker down, though.

I knew that she had heard everything Rachel and I had said and that I would have to go over and beyond to show her that I could never be that type of man to her. Trying to tell her why she was different to me would be useless because she wouldn't understand; hell, I didn't even fucking understand. I knew that my actions would have to speak for me.

As I kicked off my shoes, she looked at me curiously. I

didn't always spend the night with her because a lot of my business was handled in the middle of the night. Plus, she had already known that I had some business to take care of after the dinner we missed tonight; that business being lighting a fire under DBD to find Shug. But instead of leaving, I crawled into bed with them and spooned behind her.

I wasn't doing it to prove a point. I was doing it because in my heart, that was where I wanted to be.

# CHAPTER 14

## CAPRI

*What the fuck is going on? Is the world ending?*

"I'm so sorry to hear that, Maine."

There was no response. His tears were all that I could hear and that shocked the shit out of me. Maine had never been easy to bring to tears. He hadn't even shed a tear at his aunt's funeral. Even though he had turned into a complete son of a bitch during our break up, I couldn't help but feel mostly responsible because of my own deceit towards him. I felt guilty and was compelled to soothe him at a time like this.

"I can't believe she didn't tell me," he growled, and then I heard something crash in the background.

"Where are you?" I asked urgently.

"At her house in the garage. I didn't want her to see me like this."

"I'm on my way."

"No," he quickly insisted. "I don't want the kids to see her like this."

"It's okay. Aunt Dawn is here seeing about Nikki. I'll ask her to keep them."

"Make sure she keeps them there. Don't let her take them home," he fussed.

"I won't. See you in a minute."

I sighed heavily as I hung up the phone. I shook my head in disbelief. While doing so, I noticed how heavy it felt due to the long day I'd had the day before. I had already gone through an emotional rollercoaster all night. I was relieved that Nikki was going to be okay, I was pissed at my aunt, and I wanted to kill my fucking mother. At the same time, I was slowly falling in love with Capone as he laid in that bed with me and my kids all night, spooning with me. It was as if he was protecting us from something unknown. His presence was of disbelief to me. I wondered what I had done to deserve someone like him in my life.

As we'd laid there all night, everyone sleep around me and my eyes wide open because of the racing thoughts and diverse feelings running through me, I reminded myself that I had once felt that way with Maine as well.

My Aunt Dawn looked at me strangely as I walked into

the living room fully dressed with keys in hand. With a heavy breath, I explained, "I just called Maine to tell him what happened to Nikki. Apparently, his mother has cancer and didn't tell anyone. Now, it's in its last stage, and she's dying."

"Oh my God," my aunt breathed as she solemnly shook her head. "First, his auntie, and now this. Poor baby. You're on your way over there?"

"Yea. Do you—"

She held her hand up to stop me. "You don't have to ask me that," she said as she stroked Nikki's hair, who was lying on her lap. "I got them. Take all the time you need."

I stared at her, ready to lecture her, but I didn't even have to say anything.

"I know," she insisted. "I will not take them home. We're staying right here until you get back."

"If you need to go anywhere, call me, and I will come back."

I turned my head to avoid the look that I knew she was about to give me. I knew that she already felt really bad about what had happened to Nikki, but despite her feelings, I had to let her know that these kids and their well-being was not a game to me.

****

Thirty minutes later, I was in Maine's mother's house sitting on the couch as he lay his head in my lap. I could not hear his tears, but I could feel the moisture of them on my thighs since I was wearing shorts.

I was also crying silently. Seeing his mother in that condition was the worst thing I had ever seen in my life. The last time I had seen his mother was during the Christmas holiday. In a matter of six months, she had lost nearly one-hundred of her two-hundred pounds. The cancer was literally eating her alive. Laying in that bed was not the woman that I remembered, nor the woman that had acted as a grandmother to my kids for the past three years. In that bed was a barely breathing skeleton.

After leaving the room to allow her to get some rest, Maine told me that his mother had been blaming her weight loss and fatigue on a flu that she couldn't get rid of for the past month. He blamed himself for being too involved in his own shit to pay attention to the fact that his mother was dying. Once she'd known that she had very little time left, she finally broke the news to Maine this morning. She didn't want to go to the hospital. She didn't even want hospice. She just wanted to die in her own bed, tired of fighting at the young age of fifty-five.

"I'm sorry," I heard him say as I rubbed his head. "For everything. For not being the man you needed me to be. For not being responsible. For not manning up. I'm sorry. I'm *so* sorry."

"Maine—"

"Wait. Let me get this out," he interrupted. "The moment that I met you was when I felt like a man the most. Yes, it was because you needed me. You didn't have anything and for once in my life, I was able to give a woman something. Even if it wasn't the best, I was finally a breadwinner. I was finally the man. And the moment that you started to look at me like I was less than that, I felt like I wasn't the man anymore. I was just somebody that could be easily replaced, and that fucked with me. I was so busy trying to be somebody that I wasn't, that I didn't realize that I could still be the man in your life without supplying your every need. I stopped being *your man*, and I'm sorry."

I closed my eyes tightly, fighting the urge to break out in cries. Seeing Maine crumbled in my lap was heartbreaking. And hearing him actually acknowledge everything that I had been telling him for at least a year was a huge relief. I cared for Maine despite the demise of our relationship. I still wanted him to be a better person; if not for me, for his family and the kids that he was a father-figure for. Therefore, I was relieved that he had finally seen his flaws. I was just very sad that it had taken so much to get him to see it.

**\*\*\*\***

"Hey, Capri," Aunt Dawn answered, "How is she?"

I sighed into the phone as I pulled away from Maine's mother's house. "Dying. She looks so bad, Auntie. It's terrible."

Aunt Dawn sucked her teeth, cursing, "Damn it. That's so sad."

Because Aunt Dawn was like a mother to me, she had been around on holidays and had had the opportunity to spend time with Maine's mother as well.

"I'll be there in a minute," I informed my aunt. "I have to make a stop really quick."

"Okay. Take your time."

I hung up with a heavy heart. It broke my soul to see that woman fighting to live just another hour, another day, and it brought me to tears to watch Maine watch his mother die. It made me think of my mother. Even though she was a deceiving, insensitive, self-absorbed crackhead, I still needed to see her and give her a hug.

I called her cell phone, knowing that sometimes she answered and sometimes she didn't. Usually, she answered when she needed some money, so when she answered as I left Maine's mother's house and she agreed to be there when I got there, I knew that she must have been in need of some cash. Nevertheless, I was willing to give her a few dollars if that was the price of giving my mother her flowers while she was still here.

Maine's mother lived close to my Aunt Dawn on the Eastside of Chicago near Commercial Drive, so I was able to reach her house in less than ten minutes. Through the floor-to-ceiling window, I could see my mother walking about the living room, so I was relieved that she had at least kept *this* promise, one of very few that she ever had in my whole life.

As I got out of my car, I relished in the thought of going home, having a drink, taking a long bath, and going to sleep. Because of Nikki's accident, I had taken a few sick days off of work, but situations had not allowed me to rest just yet. I was even grateful that Capone was busy this evening. I could not imagine a sexually hectic night with him. I just wanted my mind and body to rest.

My mother must have heard me coming up the stairs because I could hear the latches unlocking as I walked up the porch. When she opened the door, she looked at me as if she didn't know what to expect: a lecture or a fight. I hadn't spoken to her since the day that I'd found her at the gas station a couple of months ago. But I knew that my Aunt Dawn had related to her how pissed I was that she had left the kids alone. Her doped up ass hadn't even had the decency to come to my house to see how Nikki was doing, but it was probably best that she had stayed away. Last night hadn't been the night for me to see her because I would have seriously hurt her. But it was as if God had brought us together by way of Maine's mother.

As I laid eyes on her while I walked through the door, the urge to punch her was not there. I just wanted to hug her instead. So, I did. And luckily for me, this was a day that she had actually showered, so instead of the ratchet sent of dirt, heroine and liquor, there was a soothing smell of Dove that swam through my nose as I wrapped my arms around her tightly. It saddened me that I was wrapping my arms around a frail, weak frame when my mother used to be just as healthy as I was. The drugs had turned her into as much of a skeleton as Maine's mother was, and that made my heart break for both of them even more.

My mother seemed to hesitate to return the embrace at first. I was sure she was shocked, but it only took a few seconds for her to return the intimacy.

After a few seconds of holding each other, she let me go in order to close the door. While doing so, she looked at me curiously and asked, "You okay?"

I sighed as I walked into the living room, and she followed. I was about to go through all the rigmarole of just needing to see her, but I wanted to take a breather first. This day had been all so overwhelming, and now laying eyes on my mother and being in this house had memories going through my brain that were making the burden of yesterday and today even heavier.

"I've been better," I chuckled sarcastically. "I need to use the bathroom. I'll be back."

She looked at me curiously as I left the living room and stepped into the nearby bathroom. Once I closed the door, I took in a deep breath and attempted to get myself together. It was always overwhelming being in my mother's presence, attempting to be mother and daughter. Except, we were two people who were actually strangers because she barely knew me, and I barely knew her, since she was hardly ever around. It was always such a struggle to have a mother who I subconsciously cared about because of who she was biologically but hated for who she was physically.

After about two minutes of collecting myself, slowing my heart rate and calming down, I pretended as if I had actually been in there doing something. I flushed the toilet, turned the water on and off, and then left the bathroom, ready to attempt to have some sort of decent conversation with my mother so that if, God forbid, what was happening to Maine's mother ever happened to mine, I wouldn't have the guilt of not at least trying.

I was confused as I walked out of the bathroom and heard complete silence.

When I noticed that the living room was empty, disappointment filled my heart. There was no need for me to look around the house for her because I saw that the front door was open. I didn't smell the scent of nicotine, so I knew that she was not outside smoking. I reluctantly looked towards the table that I had set my purse down on, saw that it was missing and instantly became enraged.

"Fuck!" I was more upset with myself than her. I knew better than to leave anything of value around her, but the burden of the day had left my guard down. "Shit!"

Luckily, I didn't have much of anything of importance in my purse but my driver's license and some cash, besides all of the clutter that is usually in a woman's purse. She hadn't stolen but about a hundred dollars in cash, and the bag was a Michael Kors that I had found in Ross. Yes, it hurt that she had stolen from me, and I worked damn hard for my money and needed it, but what hurt the most was that the moment that I had let my guard down to show her some love, she *still* allowed the drugs to lead her, instead of her motherly instincts.

"Oh shit!" I had realized that my house and car keys and cell phone were inside my purse. I began to panic.

Luckily, my aunt was one of the few people that still had a house phone, but I knew that my mother wouldn't answer the phone if I called her. Therefore, I was stranded. I didn't want to bother Capone with any more of my bullshit, especially not two days in a row. I also didn't want Aunt Dawn to have to bring Nikki out, considering the way that she was feeling. Therefore, I rushed towards it in order to call a cab. However, as I raced by the window, I noticed a big, empty spot on the street where I had parked my car.

"Fuck!" I seethed as I punched the wall. "That bitch!"

# CHAPTER 15

## CAPONE

"Gawd damn it!" Capri screamed so animatedly that I chuckled into her pussy as I continued to suck her clit. Two of my fingers had found her g-spot, and I was hammering on that motherfucker as I sucked her clit into my mouth, flicking the bud of it with my tongue at the same time.

"It's not funny," I heard her breathe heavily. "I've cum twice already!"

I temporarily let her clit go just to say, "Cum again then."

"Fuck," was her only reply in a heavy breath as she ran her fingers through my locs and over my scalp.

I was taking no mercy on that pussy.

After she had called me in a rampage when her mother stole her purse and car Saturday afternoon, I was quick to go pick her up, take her to get a new phone and take her home. But what I didn't do was stay. She needed some rest, and if I had stayed, there would have been no rest for her because I had had enough of not being inside of her.

I allowed her to rest all night Saturday and Sunday during the day, until I showed up a few hours ago after the kids fell asleep and jumped into this pussy. I had been comforting her through her drama with attention and words, but I had all plans to make her feel better with this dick, even if it only made everything all good temporarily.

As soon as she let me inside of that pussy, it boggled my mind how I suddenly felt like I was at home. Everything about this girl was driving me crazy and confusing the fuck out of me. I didn't know why I wanted to be around her and nobody else, when I had options. I didn't know why I chose to wait for her, instead of fucking one of the many women that was throwing the pussy at me. I didn't understand why I cared so much for her and wanted to be there for her. It was driving me crazy, but at the same time, giving me so much happiness that I was just rolling with it.

I had stayed in that pussy for the last hour, allowing her to cum over and over again. Then, when I finally came, she sucked me into an erection again.

Now that that pussy had made me cum for the second

time, I was eating it and her into exhaustion.

"Oh fuck!" she squealed as she began to rub her pussy against my face. "I'm cummin'."

"Mmmmm." I let out my deep anticipation for the taste of her sweet juices as I murdered that g-spot with my fingers.

"Shiiiiiiiiiiiiit!" Her juices spilled out, some splattering into my beard, but the remnants of the syrupy smell of her pussy was an erotic reminder of her throughout the day, and I often looked forward to. It was like no matter how diligently I cleaned my beard after eating her, her sweet smell was still there, and I loved it.

"Okay, baby," she begged as she pushed my head away and stopped my meal. "Okay! I can't cum anymore!"

I finally gave her relief. I left from between her legs and smacked her ass as I stood up from the bed. Even exhausted, sweating, and seemingly tortured, she looked at me and my sweaty nakedness and licked her lips.

"You better stop before I get hard again," I warned her.

"Okay, okay! I quit! Shit," she breathed as she wiped sweat from her forehead.

I demanded, "Come here," as I grabbed her ankle.

"No, Capone! I was just playing!"

I was more powerful than her though. She was a good one-hundred and eighty pounds of ass, tits, hips, thighs, and a stomach that was just imperfect enough to give her the figure of a real woman, not that fake shit on Instagram. But I was still able to pull her to the edge of the bed. Despite her fighting me, I grabbed her wrists and stood her to her feet.

"Please, Capone. I c—"

My lips on top of hers stopped her. "Shhhh! I'm playing. I'm not going to fuck you again....not right now anyway. I want you to look out of the window."

Concern filled her eyes as she reluctantly allowed me to lead her nakedness towards the window. She peered out of it and I told her, "Look down."

## CAPRI

In my designated parking spot was a shiny, silver Audi Q5 truck. The only time another car had been in my spot was when I would park in the front to allow Capone to park his luxury vehicle in the closed lot. Though I assumed, I was still in disbelief.

"You didn't," I smiled as I looked back at him. And when I saw the prideful look in his eyes, I knew. I threw my arms around him and squealed, "You did!"

"Yea, I did," he smoothly told me.

When I told him Saturday that the police had said there was little chance that they would find my car, I'd been heartbroken. Though I had insurance on my car, what they were offering me wasn't enough to get another reliable vehicle because my car wasn't worth much anyway. I really didn't want a car note, nor did I feel like the hassle of finding a reliable, affordable car, so I decided to just stay in the house during my off days, rest, and handle finding a car at another time. I had been prepared to take public transportation to work and everything. I knew that Capone would have never let that happen, though. I imagined that if he wasn't driving me around until I found a car, he would have had somebody else who worked for him do it for him. I was floored that he had gone *this* far.

"I couldn't have you out here like that, baby," he said as I repeatedly kissed his cheek.

This man was unreal. I wondered if he was like this with every girl that he messed around with. I assumed so because of the way that girl, Rachel, had acted a whole fool when she realized that he was with someone else. I imagined being in the same position as Rachel, the threat of losing all that I had experienced over the last three months, and I totally agreed with Rachel going ape shit. I would do the same. Even during our time of so much stress and drama, he managed to always put a smile on my face and put me at ease when I was in his presence. I was still very nervous about giving him my heart, but I swear he was putting in so much work to show me that giving him my heart would not be a bad idea at all.

However, even though he had purchased this truck for me, he had never mentioned being in a committed relationship with me. So I figured that it was best that I keep my heart in my pocket and just enjoy this gangsta ass, bad boy standing in front of me... And now I could enjoy this truck too!

"But an *Audi* truck?" I asked unbelievably. "I would have driven a damn Buick."

He cockily shook his head. "You deserve more than that."

I grabbed both sides of his face and kissed him with all of the passion that I had in me. It wasn't a lot, however, because he had snatched most of it all out.

Though it wasn't enough, I told him, "Thank you," wishing that I'd had enough energy to thank him with this pussy or at least some head. But my legs were still weak and my jaws were sore from the hour-long fuck session that we had just ended.

He must have seen in my eyes what I was thinking because he said, "Thank me later," and smacked my ass, which was still wet with perspiration.

As he told me, "I gotta hop in the shower," my phone rang. He went to the bathroom, and I went for my phone. I was happy to see that it was Amiyah. It had been hard to get in touch with her for the past couple weeks. I had only managed to briefly speak to her here and there, when we would usually talk every day for hours. The last time we talked had been over a week ago, and that was so odd for us.

"'Bout time you called me back, bitch," I answered.

"Don't do me," she giggled.

"What's been goin' on with you?"

"Shit," she sighed deeply. "Out here in country ass Saint Louis doing *nothing*."

"I miss yoooou," I whined. "When are you coming home?"

Amiyah sadly blew her breath. "I don't know. Shug has a real good thing going down here. I don't know when he'll be up for visiting."

"Why can't *you* come?"

Amiyah sucked her teeth. "Because he holds the purse strings, and you know he's too scared that if he let me come home alone, I won't come back."

"Urgh," I groaned.

"I know, but you a'ight. I see you all on Instagram replacing me with Eboni and Jasmine."

"I could never replace my ride or die," I said as I lay back on the bed and got comfortable.

"Damn right! So what's been going on? What's the T?"

"Girrlll..." I started. I didn't know where to begin, but luckily, Capone took long showers, so we had time to spill all of this tea.

# CHAPTER 16
*-three weeks later-*

## CAPRI

Maine's mother passed away in her sleep a week after we found out that she was dying. The past three weeks had been a blur as I juggled working, comforting Maine, helping him plan a funeral and repass, which he'd felt lost at doing, and hanging out with Capone, who had been very supportive of me helping Maine. Even after the funeral, it seemed as if Maine was leaning on me more and more, but Capone understood his loss, so supported me while I supported Maine.

"I don't even feel like going to that dumb ass party," Maine huffed into the phone.

"Then don't go," I told him as I drove towards my aunt's house.

I was pretty worn out, ready to get the kids, get home, and get some sleep. My shift had been excruciatingly long and hectic. Now that it was the summertime, the amount of accidents, shooting victims, and traumas had increased dramatically in Chicago. I'd barely had time to eat during my twelve-hour shift and my feet were killing me.

"I have to," Maine grumbled. "My family is coming in town and everything."

"But I think they would understand that you don't feel like partying. Who planned this anyway?"

"One of my cousins. She feels like after my aunt and mother's death that the family needs something to celebrate, and she is real persistent on lifting my spirits."

I laughed at his obvious irritation with her efforts. "That's sweet of her."

"I guess. That's why I'm going to go ahead and go. Are you going to make it?"

I cringed as I turned onto my aunt's block. Capone had been very understanding about me supporting Maine during his time of mourning, but I knew that Capone wouldn't be cool with me going to Maine's birthday party. Though our relationship still didn't have an official title, he was starting to be more and more inquisitive about the moves that I made. But since he had yet to establish what we were, I couldn't give him the benefit of being able to tell me where I could go. Plus, Maine had been through so much lately, and he was actually turning over a new leaf. He was the man that I had always wanted him to be; loving, unselfish and giving. He was being an awesome father-figure to the kids as well. He deserved for me to support him during this. I knew that he didn't want to be at his own birthday party and having me be there would help him turn up beyond his sadness. Plus, the only other person as close to him, Shug, was surprisingly not coming, so I knew Maine really wanted me there.

However, I still felt bad for deceiving Capone. I wouldn't be able to tell him that I was going to Maine's birthday party because I knew that he would feel some sort of way about it. And hiding anything from Capone left a bad taste in my mouth. We weren't in a relationship, but we might as well had been. Every day that we spent together, we became closer and closer. When I'd first met him, I said that I would just enjoy being single, but I hadn't even met or entertained any other man. Men would approach me, and I would deny them because even without a title, I felt kept by Capone. I felt like I was his. Plus, no other man could even compare to Capone, so why bother?

But I didn't want to be like those females who committed to a man without him committing to her as well, so I told Maine, "Sure. I'll be there."

He actually let out a sigh of relief as he said, "Thank you."

"It's no problem," I replied as I pulled up to my destination. "I just got to Aunt Dawn's house. I'm picking up the kids. I'll see you tomorrow night."

"A'ight. Bet."

"Urgh," I groaned after hanging up. For some reason, I just felt like I shouldn't be going to this party behind Capone's back, but I kept telling myself that he wasn't my man so I could do what the fuck I wanted to.

Before getting out of the car, I sent Eboni a text message, asking her if she wanted to go to a party with me tomorrow night. I felt like if I just made it seem like we were randomly going to a club to kick it, that it would be easier for me to get away with going.

She quickly replied back that she was game, so I felt a little bit better as I got out of the car. I hurried towards my aunt's house, up the porch and used my key to get in. After my mother stole my purse and car, she had gone completely ghost, so I had allowed the kids to start back coming over. Plus, I knew that my aunt had learned her lesson. She didn't want my mother around anymore either.

It was around midnight, so I knew that I was about to have to struggle with carrying the kids out to the car and getting them in the house. I hoped that Capone had made it to my condo by the time that I made it home so that he could help me get the kids inside, but I didn't expect it. Doctors had brought Fred out of his induced coma two days ago, and their entire crew was surrounding him with relief. The doctor was saying that Fred was finally healing successfully and a full recovery was looking promising.

As I walked into the house, I was both shocked and angered to see my mother. I assumed that my mother had snuck in after everyone had gone to bed and was stealing.

My aunt's first floor had an open concept, so I could see my mother's funky ass in the kitchen going through drawers. She was looking for money or anything valuable; I knew it. My aunt was loveable enough to let her sister stay with her, but was smart enough not to let her steal from her, so my aunt had sense enough to keep everything of value locked away in the closest in her bedroom.

My mother was hyper and scratching herself, so I knew she needed a fix bad.

When I seethed, "Get the fuck out," she jumped out of her skin. Her eyes bucked when she saw me, and she immediately started backing away as I charged into the kitchen. "Thieving ass. Ain't you got money left from whatever you got for my car?" Though I was pissed, my anger came out in a low growl, because I didn't want to wake the kids or my aunt with my mother's drama.

"I'on know what you talkin' 'bout," she mumbled as she cowered in the corner.

I shook my head in disgust. This was so fucking typical and sickening. "Them drugs got you so gone that you don't give a fuck about anything, not even the kids. You left Nikki and Nicholas home alone for what? To get high? She could have died! And then you steal my fucking car! Just because your bum ass don't do shit, how dare you take from me! That was my means of getting to work and taking my kids—"

"*My kids*, you mean!" she had the nerve to spit. "Those are *my* gawd damn kids!"

My eyes narrowed. "They may have come out of you, but I've been raising them! I take care of them—"

"Because you chose to!" she spat.

My eyes bucked. "Who else was going to?! You?!"

"Dawn could have. *You* wanted that responsibility, so stop throwing it in my face like you did me a damn favor. You took them because you let that dumb ass nigga kill your kids!"

Before I knew it, I had drawn my fist back and punched her in the jaw.

"Arrrgh!" She was nothing but skin and bones, so as she hit the floor, moaning in agony, I wondered if I had broken her jaw but had no sympathy for her if I had. She had said that shit to hurt me, and the fact that she *still* was trying to hurt me, after all the pain she had caused me, was fucked up. She was supposed to be my mother, not my pain, my hurt or my heartbreak.

I fought the urge to cry as I stormed out of the house, leaving her on the tile floor holding her face. I chose to leave the kids as well, opting to pick them up in the morning, because I was too enraged to deal with them.

My mother's words rang in my head, leaving me in a rage and storm of sadness. I purposely didn't think of the night that I'd lost my kids. It was too painful to relive and getting rid of the guilt had taken forever. But, instead of feeling it every moment of every day, I only felt it when my thoughts stubbornly went to that day and when I got that abortion. Otherwise, I had gone about my life like that night never happened. Those close to me knew not to mention it...*ever*.

As I ran to the truck, I allowed remorseful tears to fall. Guilt was bubbling over inside of me so thunderously that I was beginning to feel nauseous as I jumped into my truck. I gripped the wheel tightly, wishing that, back then, I had been the woman that I was now. If so, I would have been strong and responsible enough to tell Maine that he was too drunk to drive.

At the age of nineteen, I had allowed Maine to drive home after a night of drinking at a house party. I had been too scared to argue with him, piss him off and fuck up the comfortable life that I had fell into when I met him. I figured that we were close enough to the house that he'd asked me to move into a month after we met, that nothing would happen during the quick, ten-minute drive.

That night, I was six months pregnant and happy. Usually, a teenage girl would have been miserable about being pregnant at such a young age, especially with twins. But I was young, dumb, and in love with Maine. I was so happy that our family was about to begin. I had always had a strong motherly instinct because I wanted to be the exact opposite of the type of mother that mine had been. So when I learned that I was pregnant, I was ecstatic to have a chance to give my kids a different upbringing than I had. Even Maine was happy. Even though I literally got pregnant as soon as we started fucking around, he knew how I felt about becoming a mother and was very supportive of the pregnancy.

But as soon as Maine approached a red light, my pregnancy was over. Drunkenly, he ran the red light, swerved to miss an oncoming vehicle, and hit a tree. I had yet to put my seatbelt on, and the collision was on my side, so I suffered most of the injuries. He had been so scared of going to jail for driving drunk that he immediately jumped out of the car and ran. Me, being in love, painfully climbed into the driver's seat and pretended as if I had been the one driving. Though my external injuries were minor, the impact caused me to lose my babies, and I struggled with the guilt of being too timid to take the wheel from Maine in the first place. Being so in love that I allowed Maine to do what he wanted had caused the death of my children. It took me months to even get rid of the nursery that I had decorated for them in our house.

At the time, Nikki was two and Nicholas had just been born. My mother had no idea which one of the men that she had had sex with were their fathers. When they were born with drugs in their system, my Aunt Dawn stepped up to the plate, along with me, to take care of them. Luckily at birth, they both had only suffered symptoms of diarrhea, seizures, fever, sweating and vomiting due to my mother's drug use during her pregnancy.

My mother had been too worried about getting out of the hospital to get her next fix to give a fuck at any of their births. Dawn took on that responsibility, but at the time that I lost my babies, taking care of two small children had started to take its toll on her being older, tired and with less patience.

So, after I lost my kids, I happily took on the responsibility of raising my brother and sister full-time.

Fuck what my mother said; they were *my kids*. I loved them and nurtured them. I was giving them a good life and was intent on continuing to.

I started my engine and headed towards my house with tears rolling down my eyes. I just wanted to go home and get some sleep, but the moment that I woke up the next morning, I would back there for *my kids,* and they would never see my mother again.

# CAPONE

The main members of DBD were crowded in Fred's room. He was actually sitting up and talking, even cracking jokes, so I finally felt some relief after months of worrying, waiting, and praying for my nigga.

Everyone was sitting around his bed, most of us had drinks in hand. We had had to pay off the nurses a long time ago in order for them to allow us to stay in his room past visiting hours.

Everyone was smiling, especially Fred, relieved that he was going to recover. Well, everyone was smiling except for me. I was happy that my nigga had made it, but I wanted to be able to tell him that I had got the snakes that had done this to him as soon as his eyes opened, but I had failed.

When he first woke up two days ago, I asked Fred over and over again if he could recall if he knew who the nigga was that came into the trap that murderous night with Shug, but he had no idea who the other guy was.

I guess everyone could see the bitter look on my face because Omari soon checked me on it.

"Aye, man," he said lowly as he leaned into me. Everyone else around was so busy talking that they didn't hear him. "You gon' have to just let that shit go for a minute before it drive you crazy. You so focused on revenge that you ain't celebrating our nigga's life."

When I looked at Omari like he was crazy, he quickly told me, "I ain't sayin' we ain't gon' get them niggas. I'm not saying forget about it. But it's obvious that its gon' take some time. Relax and enjoy the fact that we at least still have Fred."

My fiery eyes fell on Fred's grinning face as he told Carlos, "Man, I can't wait to get out of here and get some pussy. You think y'all can sneak a bitch in here? Hell, two?"

Fred's smile was a gift. I realized that it was a blessing that he was still with us. I finally allowed myself to laugh along with him and let go of the rage. Omari was right; I needed to celebrate my nigga's life and have faith that vengeance would be mine eventually.

# CHAPTER 17

## CAPRI

"Hold up. We're going where?"

Out of guilt, I hadn't told Eboni exactly where we were going. She knew that we were going to a club, but I hadn't quite told her that we were going to Red Diamond's strip club to Maine's birthday party until we were now on our way. The look on her face made me feel worse. Then I looked into the back seat and saw the look on Jasmine's face as well. I felt like complete shit. After what had happened last night at my aunt's house, I needed this night out. I needed to get drunk and forget about my crackhead ass mama and my stupidity three years ago that had guilt swimming inside of me all day. Despite the fact that I was going to this party behind Capone's back, realizing that Maine had been a father-figure to kids that were not even his, nor biologically mine, made me feel like he deserved for me to be there for him tonight.

"Are you trying to get us fucked up?!" Eboni shrieked. "Capone is going to be pissed!"

I heard Jasmine mumble, "I ain't gettin' in trouble with my nigga ova this."

"I'm sorry, y'all, but I have to go," I whined. "And I didn't want to go alone."

"Why you gotta involve us in your ratchetness?" Eboni asked.

I giggled. "I'm sorry. He's just been through so much the past couple of months. He just buried his mother, and he has been so great with the kids lately. I'd feel bad if I don't at least show my face."

"That's exactly what you are going to do too," Jasmine told me. "*Show your face*. That's it. Have one drink and then we out. I don't like lying to my nigga—"

"You aren't lying, though. We *are* going to the club."

"To some nigga's birthday party! Girl, Omari would die."

"And so would Geno," Eboni added.

I groaned, frustrated and full of more guilt than this night had started with.

"I'm just going to say happy birthday to him, have one drink and then we can leave and go somewhere else."

Eboni nodded with her lips perched. "You gawd damn right."

If Jasmine and Eboni hadn't made me feel bad enough, as I approached a red light, I got a call from Capone.

"Hey, you," I answered through my Bluetooth headset.

"What's up? What you doin'?"

When I answered, "On my way out with Jasmine and Eboni," I heard Eboni mutter some bullshit that I couldn't make out and then laugh.

"How long you gon' be out?" Capone asked. "I miss my baby."

"You miss your baby or this pussy?" I giggled.

"Eeeew," Jasmine squealed. "TMI, bitch."

"Both. I miss my baby more, though," Capone's voice deeply and seductively wooed me. "We hookin' up later or nah?

"Hell yea," I instantly answered. "My Aunt Dawn is at my house with the kids, so we have to meet up at your house."

I was serious about my mother never seeing the kids again, so I had made Aunt Dawn babysit at my house. But it was on my to-do list to find the kids a twenty-four-hour daycare for the summer so that I could stop relying on my aunt and subjecting them and myself to run-ins with my mother. I looked forward to the school year starting so that they could start pre-school and kindergarten, then they would have a much more stable environment throughout the day.

"Bet." When Capone hesitated, my interest piqued as the light changed to green. "Look.... So me and you gon' make this official or what?" he spat so suddenly that I thought I'd heard him wrong. But I knew I had heard him right. I was so fucking happy! I felt so lucky because Capone was the shit! For him to choose to settle down with me... Me? A bitch felt like she was the shit!

But I couldn't let him know that I felt like *I* was the lucky one, so I joked, "Are you asking to marry me?"

As I drove with a smile, I felt Eboni's eyes on me. Suddenly, she and Jasmine had stopped their chatter. I quickly looked to my right and Eboni was watching my every word with this excited smile on her face.

"Not yet," Capone said with a chuckle. "But I plan to as long as you keep acting right. But in order to be my wife, you have to be my girlfriend first. A nigga ain't neva been nobody's boyfriend, but if you show me how, I'll do my best to make you happy."

I could have melted. His words hit me so hard that I even slowed down driving a little bit. But I quickly focused back on the road and simply answered, "I'll show you, baby," because I was at a loss for words.

"So it's official? You're my girlfriend?" Capone asked.

I was grinning. "Yea, it official."

"Dope," he chuckled. Then he hesitated again, and I wondered if he had suddenly felt like he had made the wrong decision. Before I could ask him what was wrong he said, "I love you, Black Beauty."

Tears, bitch! Tears! I fought to keep them from falling on my perfectly beat face. I fought to keep my voice from trembling from the overload of emotions as I told him, "I love you too," just as I pulled into the parking lot of Red Diamonds.

Jasmine and Eboni immediately started squealing.

"Awwww!" Eboni squeaked.

Jasmine shouted, "Awwwwwww, shiiiiid!"

Capone chuckled as he replied to the sound of her teasing, "Oh God. I'll let you go. Call me when you leave."

My voice was weak from appreciation and shock as I said, "Okay," and hung up.

"A'ight," I breathed. "Yea, I'mma only tell this nigga happy birthday, then we *out*."

As I parked, Jasmine and Eboni started cracking up, and I joined them.

"Yea, I bet," Jasmine said through laughs.

Luckily, Maine had a VIP list, so we were able to skip the outrageously long line that was wrapped around the club and go straight in.

♫ *I get the drip from my walk, my baby she come from up*
*north*
*My money, it come from the vault*
*I'm smoking on dope like Young Dolph*
*We touch the plug down for the cough*
*I'm sippin' on lean till I fall*
*My diamonds they shine, they Rick Ross*
*I hop in the foreign, get lost* ♫

Inside off the club, we fought to get through the thick crowd as Famous Dex blasted through the speakers. Maine had already sent me a text message telling me where his VIP section was located. As I made my way towards it, I noticed that Jasmine and Eboni were not following me.

"Y'all not comin' with me?" I asked over the loud bass.

"Heeeell nah!" Jasmine replied. "Do you know who my nigga is? I can't be seen at Maine's birthday." She shook her head vigorously. "Go say happy birthday and we'll be at the bar."

I laughed and shook my head. "Okay. I'll be back in five minutes."

They went towards the bar, and I was on my way through the tight crowd of the club to get to Maine's VIP section. As I approached the roped off area in the corner, I could see Maine standing and leaning on the shoulder of his cousin, Josh. Maine was obviously drunk already, which I wasn't surprised to see because he has been drinking a lot after his mother's funeral.

I giggled as I approached Josh, who was struggling to keep Maine standing. Maine was inches taller and pounds heavier than him, so when Josh saw me, he looked relieved.

Maine laid eyes on me, drunkenly smiled and slurred. "Hey, baby mama."

I laughed and shook my head. "Hey, Maine. Happy birthday."

"This nigga need some air. I'm taking him outside," I barely heard Josh say over the loud noise of the music and crowd.

"I'll help you," I told him, feeling relieved.

*Good*, I thought. *Now I can get out of this way easier than I thought.*

"Capri!" I heard Jasmine's voice to my left. I looked over to see that she and Eboni were rushing towards me. "We out already?"

I simply nodded, and quickly they followed.

# CAPONE

After ending my conversation with Capri, I had to sit down at my kitchen table and get myself together. I had shocked myself. I wanted Capri to be mine, but more so, I also knew that in order to be a good man to her, I had to respect her. That had meant that I had to stop fucking her without giving her the title that she deserved.

I had actually cared about respecting a woman and not hurting her, and that blew me! What further had my head gone was the fact that if I also knew that I cared enough about her to give her what she wanted and respected her, then I loved her, and that was also blowing my own fucking mind.

I had never told a woman that I loved her, and yet it had spilled out easily, like vomit, when it came to Capri. I didn't get that shit.

I guess I'd had these walls built up just to see if someone cared enough to tear them down. And Capri had definitely torn them down without even trying.

"I need a fucking drink," I mumbled with a smile on my face.

This shit... this *love*... felt good, but it was blowing me and making me nervous. I was full of all kinds of emotions.

*Oh my God*, I thought. *I have emotions.... Shit!*

I went towards my bar to make myself a drink so that I could chill out. I wasn't used to the thoughts that were running through my mind. I was worried that I wasn't going to be a good enough man to her because I had never been somebody's man before. And I was nervous that she would turn into one of those chicks that would switch up on me now that she had her title. But something in me told me that Capri wasn't a switch up type of chick. She was genuine, and she was real. I was confident that she would stay that way as I knocked back a shot of Patron.

"Omari not gon' believe this shit," I told myself as my cell rang.

I didn't plan on telling him anything right away, but since Eboni and Jasmine were with her, I knew that they were getting a verbatim repeat of our conversation, and they were going to go home and tell Omari and Geno everything.

But as I answered the phone, I realized how now knowing that she was my woman, that she was mine, I felt ... calm. I felt... loved. I felt.... whole. And that shit felt ...good. "What up tho?"

"Aye, Capone..." It was Eddie, the nigga that stayed next door to the old trap house that had seen the two dudes running out the night of the hit. He had a fucked up tone and was hesitant, so he immediately had my full attention. "I see that nigga that hit your spot. Not Rico's homie, but the other one."

Immediately, I got ready for action. I left the bar and rushed down the hall. "You sure?"

"I'm positive. When I first saw him, I knew he looked familiar. I been eyeing him all night. Then it hit me. I'm at Red Diamonds at his birthday party. Some chick invited me. She one of his cousins. I asked her did he have a homebody named Shug. She said yea, that they best friends, but Shug ain't here. I stepped outside to call you."

My heart was beating fast with eagerness of finally being able to get this nigga. "Aye, I need you to go back in there and keep eyes on him. If he leave, follow him. I got you."

"Bet."

I raced into my bedroom, and went into my closet to grab my gun and throw on some shoes. Then I rushed out of the house, jumped in my trap car, a 2013 Cadillac, and headed towards Red Diamonds.

# CHAPTER 18

## CAPONE

As Capone raced towards Red Diamonds, his cell phone rang. He was at first irritated with the interruption because he was focused on being murderous. However, when he saw that it was Eddie, his irritation turned into nervousness that he had taken too long and had missed his chance to avenge his best friend's death and his homie's pain.

"Please tell me he still there," he answered. "I'm right down the street."

"He outside. I got eyes on him though. I think he drunk."

*Fuck,* Capone thought. *I preferred the nigga be sober when he died so that he felt every bit of the pain, but so be it. Fuck it.*

"What he got on? Where y'all at?" Capone asked.

"Red shirt, leaning against a blue Escalade. It's parked in front of Hair Pros."

Capone was pulling into the parking lot right at that very moment. "I'm right here. Stay on the phone, but get out the way."

Eddie chuckled. "I'm dipped off in a corner. Make sure your aim is on point nigga."

"My aim always on point."

Immediately, Capone spotted the blue Escalade. Even in the darkness of the midnight sky, he could see the guy in the red shirt leaning against the truck as a small group stood around him. He could see no faces, but Eddie confirmed that the man in the red shirt in his sights was his target. Capone was reluctant at first because he was more thorough than this. He would have preferred not to hurt anyone in the process of killing the murderer of his friend, but this was his only chance, so he took it.

As he sped up to the Escalade, he rolled down his window, pulled out his gun, aimed and began to fire towards the red shirt. His gunshots echoed in his own ears as they filled his ears, coming through his Bluetooth headset via Eddie's call.

The packed parking lot suddenly transformed into chaos, and Capone was reminded of Miami. But despite the numerous amount of men and women who ran frantically from the gunshots and started to scream, it took seconds for

Capone to drive by, aim at that red shirt and fire until his gun was empty... and then he sped off at one-hundred miles an hour, swerving to avoid club goers as he made his getaway.

He could still hear the mayhem unfolding in the parking lot as he sped further and further away from the club. Yet, finally, after months of waiting, his heart was at ease. He felt relieved that he had finally been loyal to his crew by making this snake pay. Though Shug had yet to be found, he had at least gotten one of them, and being able to tell that to Fred and Rico's spirit was good enough for Capone.

As he sped towards the expressway, Capone heard Eddie groan through the headset.

"What's wrong? Did I miss that nigga?"

"Nah, you got him, but you hit somebody else too."

Capone could hear curdling screams getting louder and louder, so he knew that Eddie was moving closer to the scene.

"Fuck it," Capone spat boldly. "If they was surrounding that nigga, they had love for him. And if they had love for him, they needed to die too." Capone was okay with that. He was tired of his friends suffering. He was tired of sick motherfuckers causing hurt recklessly to his loved ones. Over the past couple of years, he had witnessed it too much, and he was over the gruesome ways of thirsty snakes. This would be his first innocent casualty, but he thought, *Fuck it,* as memories of Rico flooded his mind.

He felt no remorse until Eddie told him, "It's a female. Damn. Her pretty ass is outta here."

*to be continued...*

## JESSICA'S CONTACT INFO:

Amazon page: http://ow.ly/LYLEL

Facebook: http://www.facebook.com/authorjwatkins

Facebook group:

http://www.facebook.com/groups/femistryfans

Twitter: @authorjwatkins

Instagram: @authorjwatkins

Email: authorjwatkins@gmail.com

Made in the USA
Middletown, DE
08 August 2017